Hatchet

Woman Colleen Sugden

CDS Holdings

Chandler AZ

Published by CDS Holdings

P.O. Box 3178

Chandler, AZ 85244-3178

480-343-8336

Cover design complements of Dirty Bird Splattering Targets

Registered trademark of Birchwood Laboratories, Inc.

7900 Fuller Road

Eden Prairie, MN 55344

1-800-328-6156

www.birchwoodcasey.com

©2010 Fascinations. Fascinations and the Fascinations logo are registered trademarks of Marsoner, Inc., Fascinations and its affiliates in the U.S.

To my mom

Thank you for believing and for

everything else.

I love you.

Special Thanks to my editor

Tracy Peterson

tracy.peterson@cox.net

and to

my proof readers:

Jan, Linda, Randy, Ruth Ann, Terri,

Tracey & Tracy

Chapter One

Time stopped. It stood absolutely still for those few seconds when the only sound she could hear was her heart drumming in her ears, and then the stillness vanished. Everything started again in fast forward. Ani Goro's body fell forward, hitting the cement with a thump. The gun he dropped clattered loudly in the silence of the parking garage. For a moment, it seemed as though the air had been sucked out of the entire garage and then in one fell swoop came rushing back in. Samantha lowered her .45 and with dazed eyes shifted from Ani's body to where Kevin stood. He looked frozen. All animation had drained out of him, and he stared at Ani like a statue that was a lifeless part of this world.

After Samantha's pulse slowed enough to stop the blood from pounding in her head, she watched as Kevin swung his gaze away from Ani and zeroed in on her. In the jerky motion of a stone marionette or someone who could've easily been dead if not for fate, Kevin started moving towards her.

Samantha quickly sucked in a gurgled breath of air. The cement in the garage felt too close, too tight. She couldn't smell Ani's blood, but somehow in her mind, the

1

odor of blood lingered all around her—hot and wet and leaving a metallic taste on her tongue. Samantha slid into the driver's seat, securing her .45 automatic sub compact back into her holster. She wiped her damp hand on her pants leg, before turning the key in the ignition.

Caught in her headlights as the Cadillac roared to life, Kevin came to a complete stop in front of Samantha's car. His dark blue eyes were dilated so large they appeared black. He ran shaky fingers through his brown curly hair as his gaze locked with hers.

The closeness of the garage crept in around her. Her lungs felt constricted as if they couldn't get enough air. It was past time to leave. Ignoring the pain in the right side of her chest, she raised her hand in a half-wave and wheeled backwards out of the lot, stomping on the accelerator until she broke out of the underground garage and zipped onto Seventh Street. Kevin would be O.K. Ani was dead—everyone would be O.K.—now.

She rolled the window down with an unsteady hand, letting the cold night air blow on her face. She couldn't still the uncontrollable rush of jitters that surged through her body, and even though she knew it was only in her mind, the smell of blood still clung to her senses. Every move she had made these last two weeks had brought her face to face with her brother's killer, and now Ani lay dead on the cold cement in a parking garage. Good enough.

True, it hadn't been the gunfight of the century, but who would've known Ani wanted to kill Kevin? That's just it. Who would've known? Maybe saving Kevin Jacob's ass would have its rewards—like keeping her boss, Brody Thompson, from ripping her head off. Yes, that would definitely be one reward; the thought of seeing Kevin in his boxers again that also seemed like a reward. She flipped the heater on to even out the temperature as the cold December air whipped around her head.

Her lead foot now showed eighty as she raced down the freeway for home. She lifted her foot, slowing the car to a reasonable sixty-five. Jack, her partner, often preached to put the car on cruise control after a shootout. He said it would save her ass from getting pulled over— Jack and his Hitman's Creed of Wisdom. Samantha rolled her eyes. Maybe he should write a book. Cruise control took the fun out of driving.

Reaching her hand inside her jacket, she pulled out her phone. Even set on silence, the phone lit up, showing an unlisted number. Knowing full well, it could only be Kevin; she tossed the phone into the driver's seat.

Each mile she put between herself and Ani helped to ease the racing of her heart, but she still felt like she might explode. A little bit of space that was all she needed—the chance to take a breath and let her racing mind slow down to a level that might be capable of thought.

The Cadillac sped down the freeway away from Ani, away from death and hopefully towards safety. Lights from the poles along the freeway kept the darkness at bay. Thoughts of Kevin and why Ani had tried to kill him clouded her feelings of security. Her one goal of eliminating her brother's killer now didn't seem to be enough. Did she have to continue killing people to keep Kevin safe? If she did continue to kill people, was there a line or a limit, or did she simply not have one?

The subdivision of her new home on Happy Valley Road reeked of families tucking their kids into bed by eight and going to bed themselves by ten for the next day's grind. Would she ever have a chance at a life like that, or would life always consist of eating tacos with Jack and listening to him nitpick her survival skills?

Pulling into the two car garage of her spanish style house, she parked the CTS Cadillac next to the black GMC dual-cab pick-up. Samantha sat perfectly still, waiting for the garage door to close and her thoughts to stop spinning. Take deep breaths she told herself. When the shaking of her hands subsided, she stepped out of the car. Her boot made a clicking noise on the concrete floor, sending cold shivers up and down her back. The overhead garage lights lit up the entire space, and not even the scurry of a mouse could be heard. Most likely there were no mice. The place had been completely empty and sterile when she moved in a week ago.

Moving silently towards the door to the house, she flipped on the light switch, knowing the timer would go off soon and plunge the garage into darkness. Maybe she should disconnect the light from the garage door opener, so when she opened the garage, the light wouldn't illuminate her vehicle. Of course, how creepy would that be to come home to a dark garage? It could attract even more attention than leaving things alone. She shook her head. Over thinking things never brought about a solution.

She climbed into the bed of the truck, raised her arm above her head and pushed on the ceiling. A one-foot square lowered, exposing a small cubby. Immediately after Samantha had moved into the house, Guissepe and his son had installed a few convenient cubbyholes. Guissepe managed the mansion for Mr. Thompson. He made sure the overall picture ran smoothly.

Samantha extracted a license plate along with the tools she needed, pushed the ceiling back into place and climbed out of the truck. She had never replaced a license plate before, but tonight was turning out to be a lesson in firsts. Ani was dead by her own gun. That thought became lodged in her mind and rolled around as if it refused to sink in. Maybe she had built him up in her head by thinking he was unstoppable. As it turned out, anyone could be stopped. Ani wasn't the number one hitman in the country anymore. So did that mean she was? And who would want to be that anyway? Did seeking revenge for her brother somehow turn her into a monster?

Switching one license plate for the other, she screwed the old plate into a vise. A remnant from the last occupant the workbench wobbled a little as she made sure the vise remained steady. Several clicks into it she got the blow-torch going and incinerated the old license plate. She carefully put all of her tools back into the cubby. The bits of the license plate that were left she ended up leaving in the vise. What was she supposed to do with the leftover bits of a license plate anyway? Throw them in the trashcan like normal garbage, or bury them in the backyard and hope the cops didn't run out into her yard with a metal detector.

Samantha quietly pushed open the door leading from the garage to the dining room. She poked her head inside and scanned the house slowly for any signs of life. Even in the dark, the house look deserted—no pictures, no decorations and no mail. Most of the people she knew were dead, so Christmas cards were a thing of the past. It took awhile for her eyes to adjust to the darkness after being in the brightly lit garage. Maybe some night-lights would make living here easier.

The moonlight from the backyard pooled on the bare floor of the dining room. Since it was only her, she hadn't bothered to get a dining room table yet; instead she made good use of the bar stools at the kitchen counter. From the dining room, she could see the couch underneath the window in the living room. The need to search the entire house and poke her head under the bed seemed fleeting. Sometimes it was creepy living alone and being paranoid.

She slipped her hand under her jacket to feel the comfort from the cold steel of her gun as she crept from the dining room into the kitchen. Opening the refrigerator door, revealed the fact that there was absolutely no food in the house—Samantha's stomach growled in protest. She longed to be at the mansion where Maria, the cook, would have all kinds of leftovers waiting.

A cricket chirped from inside the house, and her heart lurched. The fact that Ani probably lay in a morgue by now did little to relieve her anxiety level. The man who haunted her nightmares no longer walked the earth. She wondered if she would still wake up in a cold sweat after hearing big heavy footsteps and the sound of a door crashing in. Reliving the day her brother died wouldn't fix anything, but one thing rang true. After tracking down Ani and working day after day with killers, it became clear that someone other than Ani had ordered the hit on her brother—and that someone was still alive. Ani had simply been the device to achieve the means.

Slamming the refrigerator door shut, she headed down the hall, peeling off her silk jacket as she went. The bare light bulb in her bedroom blazed down on the white haven: white walls, white comforter and white tile. Would she ever get to that point in her life when flipping on a light would reveal a picture of someone she loved, or had her new lifestyle malignantly cut out those kinds of relationships? It was good she had no one close to her. If you have no one, then no one can be taken away. She knew the lie the moment it scrambled around in her head, but she didn't want to admit she cared for Kevin or for Jack.

Meticulously hanging her jacket in her closet, she drew her gun out and slipped the holster off of her shoulders, dropping it onto the floor. She crossed the room to the bathroom, locked the door behind her and placed the gun on the counter. The reflection that caught her eye was of a pair of blue eyes, which looked way too red. She ran her fingers through her short blonde hair; trying to ignore the fact, that it didn't quite conceal the beating she had taken last week from some guy in Mexico who hadn't lived long enough to finish the job. O.K., so she might owe Jack for that one. Her finger touched the corner of her eye where an imaginary crow's-foot would be. Technically at twenty

-four, the chance of having crow's-feet appeared to be slim, but the sheer amount of stress lately would be enough to put some serious lines on her.

Turning away from the mirror, she started the shower. It always seemed to clear her head. The water felt so hot, it almost boiled everything away. She let the heat seep into her bones, knowing all the soap and water in the world wouldn't change her back into the girl she used to be. Did she really even want that? Two weeks ago, she had barely been able to defend herself, and she hadn't been able to defend her brother, Sam, or his friend, Eddie. Both ended up dead on the same day due to completely separate events, yet that string of events had brought her here. At least tonight, Kevin would crawl into a nice warm bed because she had been there to make sure of it.

Finally shutting off the water, she dried off and wrapped a white fluffy towel around her. No sounds came from outside the bathroom door. Paranoia coated her with a heavy layer of fear. Her fingers gripped her gun as she opened her bathroom door. Listening carefully, before tip-toeing across the tile floor to the closet, she caught sight of a large man standing in the doorway of her bedroom. With a racing heart, she spun her gun in the direction of the door, but it was too late. The moment she recognized Jack, leaning against the door jam, her towel went south. For a split second, she remained frozen; then dropping to

9

her knees, Samantha attempted to wrap the towel around her and hold the gun. "You're, you're…. What are you doing here?"

"Try putting the gun down before you hurt someone— mainly me. I can't stand getting shot."

"You deserve to get shot," Samantha sputtered as she turned to the bed and laid her gun down, before fumbling her towel back around her. "What are you doing here?"

"Enjoying the view."

Sticking her chin out, she turned back around to face him, ignoring the fact that her cheeks were burning. Paying no attention to the smirk on his face, she secured the corner of her towel, by tucking it in tightly under her arm. His head nearly touched the top of the door jam, and his shoulders filled in most of the width of the doorway. She tended to forget how big Jack was because, surprisingly enough, he moved gracefully. His brownish-blonde hair held its normal skewed style as if getting a cut or finding a comb would impede its natural unruliness. A day or three days stubble on his face made him look almost dangerous except for the playful light in his brown eyes.

"Aren't you ready?" he demanded as he made his way into the room and sat down on the bed.

Samantha huffed, "I already took care of Ani, so you can take your happy ass and kindly get out of my house."

Jack's head snapped up as if she had hit him. "You what?"

"I went to JS myself and intercepted Ani from blowing Kevin away."

Jack pulled a pack of cigarettes out of his front shirt pocket.

"You can't smoke in here," Samantha said, attempting to snatch the cigarette out of his mouth.

Jack swung his head out of her reach and brought out his lighter. He lit it, inhaled deeply and then blew the smoke away from Samantha. "Did you know Kevin and Becki broke up?"

Moving her gun out of the way, she sunk down on the bed beside Jack. "No, I didn't really talk to Kevin. I had my hands full, trying to take care of Ani."

Jack nodded. "I guess you did at that." He took another drag and then dropped his ash on the floor.

"What are you doing?" Samantha screeched.

"You need ash trays." Jack scratched his head as if the whole affair weighed heavily on him. "I got things to take care." He got up, ruffled Samantha's hair with his hand and started for the door.

"What things?"

"Things." And then he was gone.

Samantha sat on the bed as Jack's footsteps retreated, and the front door closed behind him. She heard the dead bolt snapping into place when he locked the door. So Jack used a key to get in. Fantastic, maybe she could leave a few more copies at a truck stop. With a huff, she got toilet paper out of the bathroom and wiped up the ash. What a pompous ass dropping ash on her floor! She checked her phone for messages and turned the volume for the ringer back on. Then she pulled on her boxers and a tank top and crawled into bed, making sure her .45 was right next to her. She hiked the covers up around her neck, wrapping one hand around the butt of her gun. Maybe she would be lucky and not dream at all tonight. How twisted things had become. Had fate brought her full circle now, ending with the death of her brother's killer? Sam's words still rolled in her mind.

She remembered walking into her mother's apartment right after the funeral when the phone rang. "Sorry I couldn't make mom's service, but I got a really good thing going on here. Come to New Orleans. It's a sure thing."

No, brother, nothing is a sure thing. She rolled over, ignoring the bitter taste in her mouth.

Chapter Two

The sharp ring of a phone pierced her dreams. "What?" she snapped, placing the cell phone to her ear.

"Which do you like better Delaware Dream or Missing Miami?"

She sat up in bed, swinging her feet onto the tile floor. "I thought you had a sure fire system for picking the ponies?"

"Yeah, but every once in a while, it's a close call, and I have someone give me random advice. Today, it's you."

"If I pick right, do I get to sleep in?"

"Look, sunshine, it's four in the morning; I can't let you sleep all day. I need you to go to the airport and pick up a Mr. Jay Holiday, terminal 3, flight six-ninety-eight at 5:15 a.m. He'll meet you at the baggage terminal." Guissepe's voice dropped, "Someone iced Ani, while he was marking Kevin. Everyone around here seems to think it was you."

"Missing Miami." She clicked the phone off. Guissepe was famous for knowing everything that went on inside and outside of the mansion. The only other person to rival his status was Cynthia, Mr. Thompson's girlfriend. Rumor had it Cynthia spent hours watching the house video monitors.

Samantha scrunched her toes and scampered across the cold tile floor to the closet. Living in Phoenix, anything cold was a luxury, according to Jack, anyway. Both sides of the closet held meticulously organized work clothes— on the left side hung grey pantsuits and on the right black pantsuits. Black boots and running shoes lined the closet floor. Dressing quickly in a grey silk shirt with a matching suit, she tucked her knife blade into her boot and strapped her holster on, before sliding into her jacket. At the airport, she would have to take her weapons off, but there was no way she'd be caught leaving the house naked.

The early morning air had a nice chill to it. Darkness lay over the desert floor broken by subdivisions popping up here and there. For the most part Phoenix was flat, but her home and Mr. Thompson's mansion were surrounded by rolling hills. The only good thing about being up this early was avoiding the traffic. The airport lay close to downtown, which could cause slow going if trying to get there during the rush hours.

Mr. Thompson undoubtedly knew of her marking Ani Goro, but what bothered her was why Kevin had been at JS. Supposedly, Ani Goro made hits solely for the Guerreros, and the scuttlebutt was that Kevin's fling with Becki Guerrero had recently ended. So whom had Kevin pissed off more—José Guerrero for not marrying his daughter and helping run the business or Becki acting on a jealous rage?

Holiday was a small man with a permanent twitch. His eyes found Samantha, dismissed her and began roving over a few other stragglers who had been lucky enough to come to the airport at 5 a.m.

Maybe it was the mean streak in her. She didn't wave or smile; she waited. Without ever seeing a picture of him, she knew exactly who he was. He was the guy in the wrinkled conservative brown suit. Expensive suit, but he'd been up all night, sweating his balls off, trying to decide what to do. He clutched the briefcase in his right hand and mopped his balding head with his left. Samantha never knew if it was because she was a girl or if some other less apparent reason made her so obscure. His eyes slid past her again. Finally, his hand began to shake as he reached inside his jacket for his cell phone.

"Mr. Holiday," she said, throwing him her best smile and extending her hand. "I'm ready when you are."

"Oh," he said, pushing his glasses up on his nose, "didn't expect a woman."

"Most don't. You have any bags?"

"No. Shit, I don't believe…. I mean does Mr. Thompson think this is some kind of joke? I didn't fly all this way to get hacked off," he leaned in closer to her to keep his voice low, "in the parking lot." His briefcase now swished back and forth with agitation.

"Have it your way." Samantha turned on her heels and began walking down the terminal.

His footsteps fell in sync with hers. Silence surrounded them as they made their way down the long corridor.

"I need to use the can."

Samantha stopped right in front of him and spun around, lowering herself a couple of inches, so her face was in his. "Mr. Holiday, my job is to escort you safely to Mr. Thompson. I'm not going into the men's bathroom and neither are you. Last chance. Do you want me to take you, or not?"

"I guess I'm nervous." He pushed his glasses back up on his nose and ran his fingers through his five strands of hair. "I hope they don't kill the messenger."

Samantha raised an eyebrow and gave a small shrug. Once inside the Cadillac, she put her holster and gun back on and tucked her blade back into her boot.

"Nice," he said as his small lips turned up in the corners.

The radio helped drown out the drumming Mr. Holiday did on his briefcase. She hated being around nervous people. She missed Jack. He was always so calm—smoke a cigarette, drink a beer, shoot the bad guys, Jack.

Coming to a stop, in front of the large wrought iron gates, protruding out from the stucco walls, she waited for the gates to roll open.

"Nice place," Mr. Holiday said as they wound along the brick road through the large australian bottleneck trees with limbs that drooped heavy with leaves. The mansion itself was a combination of brick and glass jutted together at weird angles.

The garage door opened, and they slid from light to dark as they sloped down into the massive underground garage. Samantha wondered if they would ever trust her with gate and garage codes. Maybe they were waiting to see if she could operate the elevator first—which would probably be a smart idea.

"Before we take the elevator up, Mr. Holiday, I should pat you down."

"You're kidding right. We were at the airport."

"Not kidding. Put your hands on the roof of the car." She patted him down, methodically grabbing his nuts to make sure nothing had been hidden.

Mr. Holiday came unglued. His hands came off the hood, and he started dancing and sputtering, "You can't grab a guy. That's harassment. Are you crazy?"

Samantha shrugged nonchalantly. "Ever hear the story of Benny Barbutcha? He killed a head boss after being patted down because he had a gun taped to his johnson. So now everyone gets the Benny Barbutcha treatment. Could you open your briefcase?"

Jay gave a disgusted snort and snapped open his briefcase. "I'll have you know I knew Benny. He was a loon—completely out of his mind. I can't believe anyone would've hired him, but I think he was somebody's cousin."

They passed Kevin's Mercedes on the way to the elevator. Mr. Holiday slowed his pace, keeping his eyes glued to the car.

"Something wrong?" Samantha asked as the doors closed. The elevator began to rise without Samantha touching the buttons. Someone was definitely pulling the strings today. It added to the already bad feeling she had about last night.

Jay Holiday solemnly shook his head. "You ever do any moonlighting?"

Samantha's eyes widened. "You know I can't do that."

Jay smiled bleakly. "I feel like I need a bodyguard." He ran his fingers through his hair again as if it might have disappeared recently.

"That's what I'm here to do Mr. Holiday. We made it from the airport to here with no problems."

He shook his head sadly as if the point was moot.

As they shuffled off the elevator, they were scrutinized with Bruno's cold stare—the shadow behind the man. He did everything for Mr. Thompson: secretary, bodyguard and airplane pilot. Bruno sat behind a new age desk with an ultra thin counter made of marble. Classical music rose faintly from the CD player on the shelf behind him. The crisp white long sleeved shirt he wore hid a body covered with tattoos, but nonetheless a certain aura of menace surrounded him, which no amount of polish could ever cover up. It wasn't so much his size. For in reality, Bruno stood a foot shorter than Samantha; although he definitely could have been a body builder. The fear he projected came from the eyes. It slithered in Samantha, making her hypersensitive to his dead man's stare—seeing the living as if they were dead, or at least they could easily become that way. When he spoke, his voice barely rose above the music, "Mr. Thompson is expecting both of you in the conference room."

Samantha raised her eyebrows. This was a first. She never sat in on the meetings. The conference room had not escaped the decorative hand of Cynthia. This room had a touch of the orient with silk wall hangings and a large table that glimmered with a pearly sheen.

Kevin stood by the floor to ceiling windows, taking in the view of the backyard. He turned, keeping his hands in his pants pockets. As usual it looked like sleep had eluded him. It gave him that vulnerable ragged look with faint circles under the eyes, and sometimes the eyes themselves appeared a little too bright. Samantha gave him a half-crooked smile, kicking herself for being drawn into the same attraction every other female on the planet had been drawn to—male vulnerability. Kevin may be tired, but she doubted if he was truly vulnerable.

Grabbing a chair next to Mr. Thompson, she focused on the papers he and his accountant had spread out on the table. They were so engrossed they never looked up. Mr. Holiday stood across from Samantha, carefully placing his briefcase on the table as not to disturb the conversation in process or maybe hoping he could disappear in the background with no one noticing.

Kevin brought a cup of coffee around, putting it in front of Samantha. "Thanks for covering my back last night."

"No problem. Get shot at a lot lately, or was last night an exception?"

Kevin gave her a quick smile and took the seat next to her.

Mr. Thompson looked up. "This is my accountant, Anthony Canale, and this is Samantha and Mr. Holiday." Mr. Thompson leaned back in his chair, popping his knuckles. "Well," he demanded of Mr. Holiday.

Jay Holiday swallowed hard and sprung the locks on his briefcase. He took out a ledger and handed it to Anthony Canale. "These are the records of the laundry houses used to wash the profits split between Sal Terrano and Mr. Thompson. The one on top, however, is the file I came across yesterday afternoon. In it is an itemized account of monthly receipts received over the last five months for that particular laundry house. This laundry site is one of the new houses ..."

Mr. Thompson cut him off with a growl, "What new houses?"

"The four new houses put into operation this year," Jay said quickly. "In each case, concerning the new laundry houses, I haven't been able to obtain any financial records until yesterday."

"Kevin, what in the hell is he talking about?" Mr. Thompson asked again, completely ignoring Jay.

"There are no new houses," Kevin said, clicking his cell phone open and dialing. "I'll get Sal on the line."

"Sal already knows about the houses," Jay said, clearing his throat. "I questioned Sal months ago as to why the laundry houses were drawing less, and Sal explained the four new houses were drawing some of the income. The money is going into a special account for the Juarez project." Jay opened his mouth, closed it and took his seat.

Kevin and Mr. Thompson stared at each other. Kevin held the phone up to his ear. "That's exactly what I'm thinking. How is it there are four new laundry houses that nobody knows anything about?" Kevin tapped the end of his ballpoint pen. "No, Sal, I need to know right now why there are new houses and a Juarez project that nobody on this end has even heard of." Kevin shook his head. "No way. You better get your ass up and get me some paperwork. I don't know; anything you can find." He clicked the phone off and looked Jay Holiday up and down.

Jay's eyes met Kevin's and then dropped to the table.

"You already know what Sal said?" Kevin's voice flowed with a tranquil smoothness.

"I've spoken with Sal quite a few times over the last five months, but that's why I'm here, Kevin. That story didn't sit right with me. That's why I practically broke in to get those records yesterday." Jay pushed his glasses up on his nose.

"What in the hell is he talking about?" Mr. Thompson demanded.

"Sal says I initiated the opening of those houses and that the whole Juarez project is my idea. This leads me to believe, we now have a reason as to why Ani Goro tried to shoot me in the back last night. Anthony, hand me those records."

Anthony, who had been absorbed in the documents, pushed the papers across the table to him. Kevin studied the contents, finally raising his eyes. "So if there are four of these houses, then a rough estimate would be twenty million dollars." He closed the ledger, flipping the pages idly with his thumb.

Mr. Thompson hit the intercom button. "Bruno take Mr. Holiday to a room downstairs. He's going to be staying with us for a while."

Jay's eyes seemed to pop out of his head as he regarded Bruno casually standing in the doorway. It would be the same reaction anyone would have if he or she had to be escorted by Bruno. The only thing missing was the pee that should have been running down his leg by now.

"Kevin, you and Anthony go have breakfast."

Samantha watched them leave with a sinking feeling. Not only was she going to get reamed for last night, but now $20 million dollars was also missing. She refused to let her foot tapping give her nervousness away.

The silence became deafening as Mr. Thompson leaned back in his chair, drawing in a long breath. "Every business has thieves. This business is no different. What I have to know is that the people who work for me are loyal. Are you loyal, Samantha?" Mr. Thompson's grey eyes glinted like piercing steel.

"I was taking care of personal business last night."

Mr. Thompson bit his bottom lip. "You know with Kevin dead, this whole laundry house business would have easily been framed on him."

Samantha shook her head in agreement while her foot tapped thin air.

"Take Jack with you and go over to Ed McKay's. Ed was supposed to meet with Kevin and Ani Goro last night, but he never showed up. Stake the place out. I want to know if he's in on this or not." He handed her a piece of paper with an address written on it.

Samantha pushed her chair back ready to get the hell out of there. Just as she approached the door, she heard him call her name, hindering her escape. She turned to face him.

"Samantha, vendettas always get people killed. I need you to concentrate on the job at hand."

She nodded and left.

Chapter Three

With a shaky finger, Samantha pushed the number three and then the one for the first floor. She leaned her head against the mirrored wall of the elevator, letting the air she had kept pent up whoosh out of her as her whole body slumped with relief. Putting some distance between her, Mr. Thompson and especially Bruno did wonders for her mental well-being. She couldn't help but imagine Bruno coming at her with a switchblade in each hand as the soft strains of classical music kept time with his deadly strokes. Bruno had been kind enough to provide her first and only knife fighting lesson—one that she wouldn't soon forget, or care to remember, for that matter.

The elevator door opened into the hall on the first floor. She stepped into the small hall and stopped, but she couldn't hear anything except the rustle of paper and the clank of a pot in the kitchen. The smell of fresh brewed coffee and bacon frying caught her attention, causing her to quicken her pace. As she rounded the corner from the hall to the den, her focus was diverted by a sparse, tiny Christmas tree that had been decorated with beer cans and Christmas lights. The green, red and blue lights bounced off the beer cans, giving the tree a celestial glow. Samantha shook her head, knowing it had to be the handy work of a genius. The most likely candidates would be Jack, Ken, Allen or Bruno. Samantha let out a thankful sigh that she didn't have to live here with them.

Her footsteps echoed in the empty den as she padded her way across the saltillo tile to Jack's bedroom door. Either the guys were still sleeping, or they had left early. The brown leather couches, pool table and large screen T.V. screamed man cave, but the eight-foot white monstrosity of a Christmas tree told a different story. The contrast between the two trees made her shake her head, wondering how much alcohol had been involved with that decorating party.

Pounding on Jack's door, finally brought around the groan she wanted. At the sound of the second groan, she set off towards the kitchen for another caffeine fix. This was Guissepe and Maria's headquarters—the central hub of the mansion. Samantha could see the sun glistening on the freshly watered grass outside the kitchen windows. The leaves of the australian bottleneck trees shimmered in the slight breeze. Guissepe, like every morning, had his nose hidden behind the racing form while Maria stood over a large pan of delicious smelling bacon.

"I thought you already picked today's winners?" Samantha asked, pouring herself a cup of coffee.

The top of Guissepe's silver head nodded. "I think Missing Miami is going to get dogged, but I already put my money down."

"Good to know you have confidence in my choices." Samantha pulled out a wooden chair and sat down at the table with Guissepe. "How much do you bet a day?"

"Don't ask," Maria snapped. "It's enough to give a normal person a heart attack, but win or lose he gets up the next day and starts all over again."

Guissepe winked from behind his wired gold rimmed glasses. They perched on his nose perfectly, adding even more to his grandfatherly persona.

"Are those new?" Samantha couldn't remember seeing them before.

"Huh." Maria brought over toast and set it in front of Guissepe. "He backed into Ken and Allen's car before he would admit his eyesight might be going."

Samantha felt a hand squeeze the back of her neck. She knew without looking that it was Kevin. Damn him. She kept her eyes on Guissepe's paper as Kevin slid into a chair next to her.

"I wanted to tell you thanks for last night."

Samantha gave a half-hearted smile. "It's what any girl with a compact .45 would've done." She didn't want to look directly into his eyes because something about the black outer ring of his blue eyes always made her stare too long; instead she focused more on his nose and mouth. Big mistake. His nose was perfectly straight and sat right above well-formed lips. His skin had that warm olive color that made her wish she could reach over and take his brown curly hair out of his white shirt collar. Her heart was beating a little too fast. Turning her attention back to her coffee cup, she tried not to think about how much she wanted him.

"Cynthia thinks you should come for dinner tonight at eight. She's making shrimp gumbo and a couple other Louisiana dishes. She also said to dress formal. She gets bored." He rolled his eyes and shrugged his shoulders. "See you tonight," he said, rising from his chair and planting a kiss on the top of her head.

Samantha remained motionless, at last glancing in Guissepe's direction, who was graciously studying the racing form.

"A little early for kissy, kissy don't you think?" Jack's voice cajoled her from behind.

Samantha's fingers clenched around her coffee cup. "It's only early for you Jack because you sleep in all day." Jumping up from her chair, she dumped her coffee in the sink and snatched an apple out of the basket.

"No breakfast?" Maria clucked her tongue. She put her hands on her hips and shook her head, causing her curly dark hair to swish against her coral shirt.

The smell of coffee, eggs and bacon made Samantha's stomach growl, but her cheeks still flamed from Kevin's quick kiss. "No thanks," she said, trying to escape the kitchen before anymore comments could be made.

"Oh, so now you're pissed, and I don't get any breakfast." Jack grabbed a soda out of the fridge and followed Samantha into the hall.

Samantha found the hidden elevator button. It was disguised as part of a flower in a vine mural that twisted from the floor all the way to the second floor landing with little purple flowers delicately interlaced, making the perfect hiding place for the elevator button. Stepping inside, Samantha's finger hovered over the numbers. What a pain trying to remember all the codes for each floor.

"Twenty-two," Jack said as he crowded into the elevator with her. "Where are we going, anyway?" He popped open the soda, guzzling half of it down.

"Ed McKay's place—he's the owner of JS."

Jack downed the soda and burped as he trailed behind Samantha in the garage. "What's your hurry—need to go shopping for kissy boy?" He began making sucking sounds as he jerked open the passenger door to the Cadillac. He shot her a huge grin, before sliding into his seat and pulling sunglasses out of his leather jacket.

Samantha snapped her head in Jack's direction and then rolled her eyes at his appearance: his brown hair stuck up at odd angles, his eyes looked so red someone might have mistaken him for a vampire and the three-day stubble wasn't adding to the image. "Late night?"

"It's always a late night." He flipped down the visor and examined his hair in the mirror, trying to get pieces of it to lie down, by licking his fingers and pressing them to his scalp.

Samantha hit the gas pedal, sending the car shooting into reverse and knocking Jack back into his seat. She tried to keep the corners of her mouth from tugging upward. "Last night Ed McKay, Kevin and Ani were to meet at JS. But Ed never showed up, and that's when Ani tried to put a hit on Kevin in the parking garage. Mr. Thompson wants to know if Ed was involved with Ani's attempt to kill Kevin."

Jack stopped primping. The dark brown tufts of his short hair still stuck out around the ears. "So when did you get so tight with Kevin?" Jack reclined his seat and laid back.

"We're not tight," Samantha heard her voice rise to a high squeak.

Jack snorted, "Keep in mind Kevin is smooth, and with Becki out of the picture, he's looking for a new piece of tail."

Samantha shot him a venomous look. To her annoyance, she couldn't tell if his eyes were open, or not under his sunglasses. All the air inside her lungs had escaped at the thought of Kevin not having Becki dripping off of him like skanky slime. Had Becki ordered Ani to kill Kevin? Could she be deranged enough to kill someone because he broke up with her? Nothing made sense.

"How do I get to this address," she asked, handing Jack the piece of paper Mr. Thompson had given her.

"You know how to get to the 17. So hit the 101 East right away, and that will take you all the way to Scottsdale. Exit Tatum and turn left. Third street on the right."

Samantha sped out of the gated security of Mr. Thompson's mansion and was pretty sure Jack fell asleep before they got a mile down the road. His head thumped against the window with every bump in the road. Grey and silver shrubs dotted the hills along with a few cacti and scraggly looking desert trees.

Skirting around most of Phoenix, the view consisted of desert and housing subdivisions. The freeway cut through a few low hills as she drove in silence, listening to Jack snore. As soon as she entered Scottsdale, the landscape began to put on a show with palm trees, agaves, bougainvilleas and lantana. Everything was lush as if the desert tried to push in, but couldn't quite make it. She drove up and down Cimarron Road but couldn't find an address on any of the estates. How did the postman deliver the mail?

"It's right there," Jack said, pointing to a two story brick house set at least half an acre away from the road.

Parking on the street twenty-feet from the main driveway, Samantha studied the white wrought iron fence and green lawn that led all the way up to a circular drive. "Nice place for a club owner don't you think?"

Jack took his sunglasses off. "Too bright for me," he said, sliding them back on. "It's nice, all right. I imagine JS makes good money—what with the swinging and gambling going on there. So is that where Kevin took you for your first date?"

Samantha ignored him. "Try to keep your eyes open, and how did you know this was the house?"

"I know things." He rolled down his window to blow his cigarette smoke outside—his way of being considerate.

Samantha wrinkled her nose at the smell. She started to tell Jack not to smoke in the car and then considered being stuck in a car with him and no nicotine. "Maybe we should go in," Samantha suggested, beating a pen against the steering wheel.

"No way, I got a bad feeling about this one. We'll wait."

Jack plucked his phone out of his pocket. The little phone vibrated in his large hand. "What?" His jaw tightened, compressing his lips together. "I told you that last night—put an ice pack on it, take care of business and don't forget an anti-inflammatory."

Samantha strained to listen to the conversation, but whomever Jack was talking to she couldn't hear their voice.

He hung up, shoving his phone back into his denim shirt pocket. "What?"

"I just wondered ..."

"Bruno, he has lower back problems." Jack finished his cigarette and flicked it out the window.

"I didn't realize there was a doctor in the house."

"Huh, little do you know. Now keep it down with your rat-a-tat-tatting. I'm going back to sleep." He reclined his seat, shifting around until he got comfortable.

Samantha tried not to tap the pen against the steering wheel but this sucked. Nobody at the estate came in or out—the grass grew, the birds chirped, and Jack snored. Once in a while, a hummingbird flitted into the nearby eucalyptus tree and gathered leaves for a nest. Even the clouds refused to co-operate with entertaining her. One or two light and fluffy clouds drifted overhead, and other than that the sky remained perfectly clear.

The morning dragged on until the sound of a siren brought Jack up out of his seat. He listened, cocking his head out the window as the siren wailed again. "It sounds like they're coming closer. Make a large block and see what happens."

As soon as Samantha started the car and pulled away from the curb, a police cruiser zipped up the street behind her, turning into Ed McKay's drive. "Call Guissepe and see why the cops showed up," Samantha said in a squeaky voice as she drove slowly—careful not to draw any attention to them. She cruised through the subdivision while Jack waited impatiently for Guissepe to get him some information. Meandering through back streets, she finally ended up on Scottsdale Road. Her stomach growled when she saw a fast food dive. If only she could've had a signature BLT made by Maria back at the house; instead she pulled into the drive-through and decided on a breakfast sandwich.

Jack ordered burritos as he waited for Guissepe. He let out a "uh-huh," and clicked the phone off. "Guissepe says a call went into the police saying Ed McKay was found dead with a bullet in the head. Mr. Thompson wants us to pack it up for the day."

"Do they know who killed him?"

Jack shook his head no as his mouth inhaled food at a rapid rate.

"You want me to take you back to the house?" Samantha asked, pulling out into traffic.

"Why? Where are you going?"

Samantha bit the inside of her bottom lip. "Nowhere. I have a couple of errands."

"Maybe I should go with you, you know, to help you buy a dress that isn't black or grey. You dress like you're in mourning."

Samantha felt the heat of her anger rise all the way up to the top of her head. What the hell did Jack know about mourning? She sucked in a breath and narrowed her eyes at him. "I'll have to decline. My rule of thumb is never to take style advice from a guy with egg in his goatee."

"Suit yourself," Jack said, pursing his lips together and raising his eyebrows. Then he flipped his sunglasses back on and leaned back in the seat.

Samantha fought off the urge to blare the radio. For some reason, Jack looked like he really did need the sleep. Hadn't he got a good night's sleep, or had he been out? She studied his sleeping form. If there was one person she thought she could trust that person would be Jack, but why did she think she could trust anyone at all?

Chapter Four

Standing inside the elevator, Samantha took deep breaths, before pushing the intercom button. Her new soft silk dress clung to her slender curves, adding to her agitation. She had taken Jack's advice and picked a pale yellow dress with a low back, but she felt her confidence waning. A nice black suit with a holster and a gun would have eased some tension.

With a quick jab of her finger, she hit the button. "Hi, It's Samantha." She smiled self-consciously into the camera, hoping someone would hurry up and get her the hell out of here. The third floor was Mr. Thompson and Cynthia's private living quarters. They were the only ones who had the code for that particular floor; except maybe Kevin, who seemed to come and go as he pleased.

The elevator whizzed upward, and Samantha held her breath as the doors opened. Cream-colored couches made a semicircle around a crackling fireplace. Candles twinkled on the mantle. The room exuded a warm, relaxed feeling that did little to curb Samantha's edginess. Stepping out of the elevator onto the plush shag carpet, Samantha jumped at the sound of Cynthia's voice.

"This is my favorite room," Cynthia said as she came around the corner, carrying two glasses of red wine. She handed one to Samantha, tilting her head towards the overstuffed couches. Her dress caught the eye with an electric cobalt blue color and a slit so high on her thigh it made Samantha wonder if she wore anything under it. As Cynthia walked around the couches, her red and gold hair swayed across her bare white shoulders.

Samantha's feeling of being overdressed quickly turned into the discomfort of being underdressed. She sipped her merlot, praying not to spill any, and took a seat across from the fireplace. "Where are Mr. Thompson and Kevin?"

Cynthia shook her head and rolled her eyes. "Brody is a disaster. He is wound like you would not believe. Twenty million missing—I'll be scraping him off the ceiling for days. Anyway, Kevin and he should be in anytime. They know I don't like to overcook the food."

Samantha clicked the back of her new brown and yellow high heels together. She hated small talk. What do you ask? What don't you ask? "Do you cook all the food for you and Mr. Thompson?"

A giggle escaped her. "Maria brings up enough food for an army. To tell you the truth, I live on energy bars and water, but I like to cook for the fun of it whenever we have company. I'm so glad Kevin wanted to have you up for dinner. I thought I would puke if I had to spend another evening with Becki. There is something wrong with that girl. She never seemed quite right. It was like she attached herself to Kevin, and he never could shake her. I gave her the nickname Octopus."

"Cin …," Kevin moaned. "I give you two minutes and you're already trying to run my date off." Kevin cozied up on the couch next to Samantha, placed his arm behind her and let his fingers brush against her neck. "I call her Cin because look at her. She's Brody's downfall, and now she's trying to be mine."

Samantha forced herself to breath steadily as Kevin shot her a crooked smile. She felt a warm tingle creep through her, starting at her neck and working its way down.

Cynthia raised her wine glass to signal a toast. "I simply say what I think." Her large green eyes batted in mock defense.

"Too damn often." Mr. Thompson stalked in and headed straight for the glass decanter, which was on the shelf of the small bar by the fireplace. After pouring himself a glass full of dark amber whiskey, he turned to face the trio. "Let's eat."

Samantha let out a breath—she had unconsciously been holding in. It felt divine having Kevin's fingers trail along her neck but unnerving. He had a very sensual presence that made her not trust herself at all. Sitting on the couch made her feel trapped like a ball of energy with nowhere to bounce. She rose quickly, hoping to gain distance from him, only to feel his hands wrap around her waist from behind. She swallowed. The dress suddenly felt flimsy as the warmth of his touch burned through to her skin.

She followed Mr. Thompson and Cynthia around the corner to a small dining room with another fireplace burning cheerfully. Candles on the table and walls cast a romantic light, and the sweet aroma of clover and cinnamon filled the air. A large dark table dominated the room, offering silver dishes piled high with food. Delicate purple flowers wove their way across the table with simple elegance. A secret place where people could relax and nothing from the outside world could get in.

Kevin pulled a chair out for her. For a moment, she looked right into his eyes and a feeling of ease washed through her body that reached all the way to her toes. She hadn't experienced this in so long; it made her giddy. Maybe the wine was spiked. Dragging her attention away from Kevin, she noticed even Mr. Thompson appeared to be loosening up. If one bothered to look past his scar that started above his left eye and ran past his chin, he did have a ruggedly handsome face—expressive grey eyes, strong nose, full lips. He pushed Cynthia's chair in for her and refilled her wine with concise efficiency.

The sleeves of Kevin's white shirt were rolled up, showing off his olive skin, as he dished food out for Samantha. Before she could stop herself, Samantha reached out and ran her fingers across his scraped knuckles as he placed a buttered roll on her plate. Even in the candlelight, his right eye looked a little swollen.

Kevin's eyes caught hers before he shifted his gaze to Cynthia. "What are we having tonight?"

"A few Louisiana dishes—that's where I grew up," Cynthia said, directing her comment to Samantha. "We're having boulette, shrimp gumbo and dirty rice with beans."

Obviously, Kevin didn't want to talk about why his hands were scraped up, so Samantha kept her attention on Cynthia. "Is that where you and Mr. Thompson met?"

Cynthia bubbled, "I'm surprised you didn't hear how the two of us met, considering what a gossip everybody is in this house. No, Brody and I met in New York—very romantic, if I say so myself." She fluttered her long, dark eyelashes at Mr. Thompson. "I was dating a soon-to-be senator. Brody along with Kevin came to our house for a poker game. Well, to make a long story short, James had a terrible gambling habit, and before the evening ended, he was losing badly." She touched Brody's hand and smiled. "So Brody tells James, he'll play him one more hand—if he wins he takes me out on a date, if he loses he gives James all of his money back. It must have been love at first sight." She winked and puckered her lips in a mock kiss.

"It was babe," Mr. Thompson's voice deepened as he brushed Cynthia's lips with his thumb.

Cynthia cleared her throat and rolled her eyes. "Anyway, James took the bet and, of course, lost the hand, but his temper flared. So instead of being the bigger man, he pulled out a knife and sliced Brody's face. You can see it starts above the eyebrow and goes all the way down to his chin. We had the worst time shaving for at least two months." She gently reached up and stroked his cheek. "Anyway, Brody knocked James down, stomped him a few times, grabbed me, and we've been together ever since."

"Wow." Samantha swallowed a piece of shrimp that tasted like it came straight from the bayou. "I had no idea."

"You're a little bit of an enigma yourself. No one has ever said where you came from?"

"Now you've done it, Samantha. She won't leave you alone," Mr. Thompson said as he finished off his whiskey.

"I grew up in Florida, but lived in New Orleans a month, before I met Mr. Thompson."

"Ani was from New Orleans, wasn't he?" Cynthia asked as she peered over her wineglass.

Samantha sputtered a little on a piece of boulette. "Yes, he was."

Kevin raised his glass. "I would like to toast my two best friends in the announcement of their upcoming wedding. May your years together be long and happy!"

"Brody, you know I wanted to tell him," Cynthia said, slapping Brody's arm.

Brody shrugged, wiping his face with a white linen napkin and tossing it on his plate. "To my wife, the best cook this side of the Mississippi."

They tapped their glasses together. "Congratulations," Samantha said, slipping Kevin a small smile.

"Brody had barely popped the question to me last night when Kevin stormed in, telling us how he almost got killed." Cynthia stared up into Brody's eyes.

Mr. Thompson grunted, stood and offered his hand to Cynthia. "I hate to leave good company, but I'm going to spend some time celebrating with my lovely fiancé."

"There's dessert in the living room for the two of you. Have a good night," Cynthia called over her shoulder as she swished out of the room, never taking her eyes off of Brody.

Samantha looked at Kevin. "Is that normal behavior?" she asked under her breath.

Kevin refilled her wine glass. "I don't think anything in this house constitutes normal behavior, but for Brody it's not really abnormal. He wants what he wants and he almost always gets it."

"Is he the only one around here who has that attitude?"

"He's the only one as blatant about it," Kevin said, lowering his eyelashes over his dark blue eyes. "But the dessert is to die for, so let's go have some." He held his hand out for her.

Butterflies paraded through her stomach. Not being alone with Kevin offered the advantage of keeping distance between them. Now the feeling of defenselessness bombarded her thoughts. O.K., in fact, they had been alone before, considering they had slept together twice, but that had been sleeping—nothing else. The fireplace in the living room threw shadows against the walls, and candles twinkled adding to the dream like illusion of the evening. In the middle of the coffee table sat a large plate of cake and a decanter of wine.

He cut a piece of what looked like chocolate cake and then took a seat next to Samantha. "It's rumored if we share this cake we'll fall in love," Kevin said, placing a piece of cake on his fork and holding it out for her.

This was one of those situations when she wished Jack would come rushing through the door screaming at her to do something; instead she had to look Kevin right in those beautiful eyes and not feel like she was losing herself in them. "Really?" She bit the cake, letting the rich chocolate taste melt in her mouth.

"No, but it sounded good." He took a mouth full, settling back into the couch.

She let her body relax, ignoring the heat that seeped into her as his arm brushed against her. Maybe she worried too much. Besides, what did Jack know about dating? There was no need to run away. No outside world at all. Only Kevin and her with cake and a crackling fire to keep them warm.

"So, why were you marking Ani, or are you really my guardian angel?"

"Pretty elaborate set up to get me to talk."

He shrugged while his eyes studied her, waiting.

She looked away from him into the fire, hoping the words wouldn't stick in her throat. She closed her eyes, drumming up the courage to speak. "Ani killed my brother, and … I've been waiting for my chance. More than waiting—planning." She drew her gaze away from the leaping flames of the fireplace and focused on him. His eyes were steady and unblinking. Wiping her sweaty palms on her dress, she willed herself to relax.

"I'm sorry," Kevin put the cake down. He put his hand behind her neck and drew her closer to him. "How did it happen?"

Samantha saw Ani burst through the door and began to shiver. "My brother and Ani were partners. I stayed home from work that day because Sam was so nervous; he made me nervous." Samantha smoothed a wrinkle in her dress, taking a deep breath. "He and Ani were supposed to have some big job planned, but instead Ani came to our apartment and put four or five bullets into Sam. I grabbed a gun and shot Ani ... and then I ran." She realized a tear was streaking treacherously down her cheek. With a shaking hand, she swiped self-consciously at it. Kevin stroked her hair and tucked her against his chest.

"I'm still running. In my dreams, I see him kicking in the door and firing round after round."

Kevin wiped another tear off her face with his thumb, holding her even closer until her breathing slowed. With her head buried in his chest, the smell of him surrounded her—cool and clean, like fresh linen or lemon blossoms on a spring day.

"Come here," he whispered, rising off of the couch and disappearing through a door off of the living room.

Samantha followed, battling the vulnerability that ebbed and flowed inside of her. A large bed with a dark silk canopy sat on one side of the room, and the only light came from a fireplace at the foot of the bed. Her body tensed as she came to a complete stop. "I'm not staying the night."

He closed the door behind her with a slow solemn click and brought his hand up to her neck. "I don't expect you to sleep with me, only lay with me. Like those nights in Mexico." He kissed her slowly as his other hand guided her waist into his.

Samantha felt a fire rush through her. The kiss made her head reel as her whole body leaned into his.

Taking a step back, Kevin's breathing came out in jagged bursts. He took her hand and walked her to the bed, barely lifting her so she could sit on the edge, and kneeling down, he began to take off her satin heels. "I know what it's like to want to get revenge. My dad was shot, and I never found out who did it."

Samantha ran her fingers through his dark, curly hair. A floating sensation crept through her body, accompanied by the feeling of being safe. Somehow, she hadn't realized how badly she missed being taken care of. "How did you deal with it?"

"I finally put it behind me and concentrated on my own life, but it took quite a while. Brody stood by me, talking to me, taking me in. I've lived with him off and on since I was sixteen. This house was designed for Brody and me, but when Cynthia came along, I got my own place in New Orleans." Kevin walked around the bed. Lying down, he patted the bed, waiting for her to join him.

Her heart pounded in her chest. She unconsciously licked her lips as she studied him. The thought of him touching her again made her body scream out as if she was already addicted. Samantha snuggled into his arms and soaked up the sensation of him running his fingers through her hair. She listened to his smooth, lilting voice as he described the funeral and how he and his mom had coped. The feeling of being protected and safe overpowered her. Her eyelids drooped lower with each stroke of his hand until sleep finally wound its way through her mind, and she drifted off.

Chapter Five

The burgundy chenille blanket felt so soft against her skin she didn't want to wake up. Light from outside barely intruded into the room through the slats in the white wooden shutters. The weight of his arm across her made her want to snuggle down in the covers and never come out. Samantha rolled over and came face to face with a naked Kevin—maybe naked, maybe not. She wasn't going to find out. Could she sneak all the way out of the house with no one realizing she had spent the night? Doubtful, Guissepe watched the monitors like a hawk.

Kevin looked so sweet and innocent—all that curly brown hair falling everywhere. No wonder she got conned into staying the night. She began inching her way backwards out of the bed, but before her foot could touch the carpet, his hand grabbed her wrist and pulled her back to him.

His dark blue eyes popped open as if he had been awake for a while. "You're not trying to sneak away are you?"

"Going to the bathroom?" She smiled and batted her eyes.

"No." He put his arm around her waist drawing her up against him. He began kissing her neck until a small gasp escaped her. "Now you know how I feel," he said, letting her go and lazily watching her through veiled eyelashes.

Samantha slipped out of bed. "I feel ridiculous. I hope no one sees me leave here wearing last night's clothes."

Kevin pointed to an overstuffed red velvet chair where a brown shopping bag sat. The same style bag as the ones Cynthia used when she ordered Samantha's clothes for her.

With narrowed eyes and arms crossed over her stomach, Samantha looked down at Kevin. "Am I that easy to read, or are you that confident in your powers of persuasion?"

"Nothing of the sort." Kevin sat up, causing the blanket to fall away, revealing his muscled stomach and blue boxers. "I had Allen get those for you because I need you to be my bodyguard for a few days."

Samantha's eyebrow shot up. "I can't take off; I work for Mr. Thompson."

"So do I, but Brody wants you to be with me. He doesn't think I'm safe even though Ani is dead. I'm going to New Orleans to see if I can find out more about the fake laundry houses."

Samantha's face paled. "Why New Orleans?"

"A friend of mine, Senator McCullen, lives there. I tracked down one of the owners of the laundry houses, and the guy said that without a doubt Senator McCullen had recommended the investment. It's the only lead I have; besides the lawyer who set up the deal."

"So, it's a long shot."

"Yeah, but if we step on the right toes, it could get ugly."

Samantha blew a stray hair out of her face as she stared at Kevin. A trail of fear blazed up and down her back, causing her to break out in goose bumps. She turned and scooped up the bag of clothes as his strong brown arms wrapped around her from behind and held her close.

"And besides," he whispered in her ear, "it will give us time to be alone together."

A small sigh resonated from her throat. Kevin made her feel safe in a world she knew to be the opposite. She twisted in his arms, putting the clothes between them. "I'll be out soon," she mumbled as she slipped into the bathroom and closed the door behind her. She leaned against the door for support. How would she survive even more time alone with him? Her instincts told her to run if she wanted to keep her sanity intact. Oh, sweet sanity. Nothing had been sane for a while, and this certainly didn't look like the path to finding it.

The bathroom seemed almost as big as her bedroom at home. Large mirrors over the vanity reflected a thin girl with big blue eyes. Too bad the eyes still had yellow bruises underneath them. They matched the dress, anyway. Turning away from her reflection, she checked out the view from the oversized window above the garden tub. Seeing the hills through the green leafy branches of the gigantic australian bottleneck trees, Samantha appreciated the quiet beauty of the morning. Knowing she was on the third floor and no one would be able to see in, she peeled off her dress, opting for the shower over the bathtub with side jets. The steam washed away her residual fear of New Orleans. Superstitious—that's all, returning to where her brother had been shot and this whole misadventure had begun. Maybe it would be a chance to put to bed some ghosts. Ha. Her short laugh ended her shower.

Rummaging through the big brown bag, she found makeup and a brush. Allen must have ransacked her entire house. Taking out a grey silk suit with a white silk shirt, Samantha began to dress. Cynthia always ordered Samantha's clothes for her. There was never any indecisiveness about what to wear—grey or black suit with a white or grey shirt—done. Now her wardrobe had been upgraded to include black boots; instead of the tennis shoes that she had been forced to wear for a week with the suits. Looking inside the right boot, she found her knife carefully tucked into the small pocket in the boot.

She flipped the brush through her short blonde hair, dashed on a little makeup and folded the silk dress, placing it in the bag with her extra clothes for the trip. Pausing to glance in the mirror, she thought the suit and the bobbed hair style gave her a very professional look. The jacket fit loose enough no one would guess there was a gun underneath it.

Disappointment bloomed inside of her as she pushed open the bathroom door and found the bedroom empty. Her boots sank in the deep pile carpet as she crossed the room to the door; an eerie thought entered her head that even in boots footsteps would be easily muffled with this type of carpeting. Slipping out of the bedroom, she crossed her fingers that no one would be around.

The bedroom door had barely closed when Cynthia looked up from her book and pulled her reading glasses off. "I've been considering lasik surgery, so I don't have to wear these silly things. How did you sleep?"

Samantha couldn't decide if Cynthia asked out of sincerity or maybe jabbing at her for spending the night with Kevin. "Good. Your dinner was excellent," she said, trying to change the subject.

"Kevin looked so much better this morning. Did he tell you about his insomnia?"

Samantha shook her head, coming to a stop beside the couch Cynthia sat curled up on.

Cynthia raised her eyebrows. "He never does," she said in a lowered voice. "But believe it, or not he can't get more than a couple hours of sleep a night if he's not with a girl. I know it sounds strange, but it's true." She held up her hands in a half shrug. "I think that's why he always has a girlfriend. He needs the sleep." Her cat green eyes narrowed. "I also think that's why he and Becki were together for so long. She used to play wicked games, telling him she would show up and then showing up a day later, always with some preposterous excuse. Of course, you should have seen her when he would try to break up with her. She would freak out and throw screaming fits about how her dad wanted them to get married. She would top it off by crying her head off. Nuts!" Cynthia's red curls bounced with each head bob.

Samantha smiled and gritted her teeth. "I'm going to grab some breakfast. Tell Kevin I'll be downstairs."

"Nonsense." Cynthia jumped off the couch, grabbed Samantha's arm and began pulling her along.

Samantha kept pace with Cynthia as they went around the corner and down the hall. Patches of sunlight fell through the floor to ceiling windows onto the deep pile, off-white carpet. Samantha caught herself gawking at the acres of green lawn and the Olympic sized pool that sat right in the middle of it all.

"I had Maria bring breakfast up for us. You don't know how cooped up I get. Brody doesn't like me to leave the grounds. I get one spa day a week and that's it. No shopping. It all has to be done on-line, or someone has to come to the house. I really could lose my mind," she said, marching into the kitchen and pouring two cups of coffee.

Light bounced off the copper pots, making a polka dot pattern on the kitchen island below. A large string of garlic hung on the wall by a copper hood, and beneath the hood was a six burner stove with a double oven. Samantha ran her hand along the pale tile countertops.

"You did all the decorating?" Samantha asked in awe.

Cynthia looked over Samantha's shoulder, cocked her head and narrowed her eyes. "I try to keep busy, but the problem is I'm starting to run out of things to decorate. Right now, I can start planning the wedding. I'm thinking something outdoors with tons of ..."

Before Samantha could move out of her way, Cynthia lunged past her and dived for a fat iguana that sat staring at them from the counter.

"I hate to interrupt wedding ..."

The two-foot long lizard scrambled off the counter and shot straight up Kevin's leg.

"Hey, get this thing off of me," Kevin yelped as he began to spin around in a circle, shaking his leg in an attempt to get rid of the lizard. Kevin's face turned dark red as his whole body shimmied, trying to free himself from the little beast.

Cynthia danced around him, grasping futilely to get a hold of the lizard. "Don't hurt my baby," Cynthia screamed.

The iguana changed his mind, scampered down Kevin's leg and dashed out of the room, whipping its tail as it went. Cynthia chased after the iguana, lecturing it on how it could get hurt acting like that.

Kevin brushed off his black slacks which didn't appear to have any large holes in them. His face returned to its normal color, and he offered Samantha a weak grin. "Some kind of bodyguard you are." He gave his leg a final shake and reached for a bagel.

As her laughter subsided, she wiped a tear from her eye. "I suppose I could've shot the lizard, but I think that definitely would've put holes in your pants."

Kevin pulled her in close, kissing her neck and then whispering in her ear, "All right, you're off the hook this time." He let go of her slowly, staring into her eyes. "We need to get going."

Samantha sucked in a breath to suppress the tingling chills that now ran rampant through her body. Forcing herself to turn her attention away from Kevin, she grabbed a bagel, took as big a slurp of coffee as she dared without burning her tongue off and dumped the rest down the sink. Oh, how crawling back into bed with a warm cup of coffee seemed tempting—maybe even with Kevin.

"Your bag is already in the car," Kevin said, wrapping his arm around her waist as they headed down the hall to the elevator. "I also had Allen switch your gun—the one he found in your car. Did Jack ever switch the gun that you shot Ani with?"

Samantha shook her head. She should've thought of that, but she had been more concerned about how Mr. Thompson would take the news.

"Jack's been a little hard to pin down lately. I'm not sure where his head is." Kevin pushed the elevator button and then paused as Cynthia caught his attention. "We'll be back in time for your party tomorrow night, Cynthia," he said, hiding his grin.

Her butt swung back and forth in the air, and when she turned her head to face them, her hair stuck straight up from the static electricity of being under the couch. "You better," she mumbled, before lowering her head back down to the floor. "Come on, Tony. Mommy's not mad."

Not wanting to explain that Jack had been keeping company with Becki Guerrero to help Samantha find Ani, she switched the subject as the doors to the elevator closed. "You look so refreshed, Kevin. Did you sleep well last night?" Samantha batted her eyelashes at him. Now that the lighting was good Samantha could see bruising under Kevin's left eye, and it wasn't caused by lack of sleep.

"I can see you and Cin got to spend some time together."

"Not long enough to answer all my questions."

Kevin raised an eyebrow and gave her his full attention.

"I've been wondering how long you and Becki were together, and … did you two have an open relationship?" There she'd said it.

"Wow, go for the sucker punch early in the morning." He stepped out of the elevator into the garage, taking her hand in his. "We were together about two years and had an exclusive relationship. Why?" His eyes narrowed as if trying to read her mind.

She bit her lip. "I was curious about your relationship that's all, and speaking of sucker punch, is that what happened to you?" The limo driver stood patiently waiting for them.

"This is my pilot, James," Kevin said, nodding at the chauffeur as he slid into the back of the limo and pulled Samantha in next to him. "I'm in a lot of trouble here," he murmured, keeping his voice down. "If someone other than Brody was my boss, I'd already be dead. I have to find out what happened to that money anyway I can. These bruises are from getting the lead on Senator McCullen."

"I thought the senator was a friend of yours?"

"He is, but the guy I got the lead from yesterday wasn't."

Samantha's mind reeled with the possibilities. Could it be Becki had been up to a lot more than dating two guys at the same time? How long did she and Ani date? Could they have been working together the whole time and now wanted Kevin dead? Did Samantha dare quiz him more? Although the truth was, he most likely didn't know if Becki schemed behind his back. Out of the corner of her eye, she watched him diligently working on his laptop. That vulnerable look he always had about him must have been sleep deprivation. There didn't appear to be any sign of that now: no shadows under his eyes, no haggard expression, only a deep focus for whatever he was working on.

It didn't take long for them to reach the small airport on the north side of town. The view consisted of long rows of steel hangers housing planes, which couldn't be seen, combined with rows of open hangers, which only had a metal roof, covering the planes.

The jet was already sitting in the loading area. Samantha and Kevin climbed aboard while James parked the limo. The jet came loaded with a wet bar, mini-refrigerator, microwave and the most comfortable, beige, suede couches. "Welcome to my office," Kevin said as he stashed his laptop in one of the overhead compartments. "We'll be in New Orleans in less than three hours."

"Are we coming back after meeting with Senator McCullen?"

Kevin shrugged. "That depends. I tried calling Nathan Duvall, the lawyer who set up the contracts, but I wasn't able to reach him. We might try going to his office. I have a place in New Orleans we can stay if need be."

His voice sounded casual, but Samantha couldn't help shifting in her seat.

Chapter Six

Samantha gazed out the window of the limo at the tall oak trees lining the winding road that led to Senator McCullen's estate. Even in the grip of December, leaves still clung sparsely to the branches. Perhaps, this year would boast a warm winter.

The plane ride had been relaxing enough for her and Kevin to take a nap. She stretched her toes inside her boots in anticipation of the meeting. Kevin sat beside her with his head buried in his laptop. Sexy, the way his brown curly hair fell around his face, and Samantha had always thought computer geeks weren't sexy. How wrong indeed. Of course, she could still see the scrapes across his knuckles that told a different tale.

The trees parted in front of a two-story, white, columned home with a front porch running the full length of the house. Kevin took her hand as she stepped out of the Mercedes into the bright sunlight. Admiring the architecture of the plantation home, she had to shade her eyes from the sun to get a better view. The windows were trimmed with grey shutters on each side of them, and on the second story Samantha felt certain someone stood in the shadows watching. It could be a maid she told herself as she tried to shake the impulse to stare back. Maybe old houses automatically brought about a sense of mystery or concealment. After all, how many generations ago had this mansion been built? Still, didn't the curtain fall ever so slightly back into place?

Kevin rang the doorbell and a deep chime echoed through the house. A man with a white head of hair opened the door. He shook Kevin's hand and slapped him on the back, pulling him into a half hug.

"Senator McCullen," Kevin said as he stepped away from the elderly man, taking hold of Samantha's elbow. "This is Samantha Cross."

The grin on Senator McCullen's face disappeared into sobriety, and the sparkle in his eye shifted to calculating measurement. The moment so brief it had flitted away by the time the senator bent to deliver a small kiss on Samantha's hand. "How nice of you to bring such a beautiful lady with you. I'll have to invite you more often from now on."

Samantha smiled at the lilting southern accent. A memory of a funeral she had attended with her brother danced around in her head. It had been raining hard, and everyone had stood out by the grave dressed in black with matching black umbrellas. Whose funeral could it have been? "Nice to meet you, Senator McCullen."

"Well, come on in to the drawing room. I had Rose-mary make us up some tea. Would you like one lump or two? I always loved that cartoon," he chuckled to himself while he poured everyone a glass of iced tea. "This weather has been so unpredictable; instead of hot tea in December, we're having iced tea. Oh well, keeps us on our toes." He plunked down in a chair next to the unlit fireplace.

Samantha took her tea and sat on the floral couch across from him. The room had a touch of Victorian with flowery wallpaper and wood floors. A large chandelier hung above their heads, casting drops of light onto the high-backed, purple, velvet chairs.

"How's Maggie? She's Senator McCullen's wife," Kevin said as he took a seat so close to Samantha that their legs touched.

Why had he sat so close? She tried to ignore the heat that began to creep through her body. Returning the senator's penetrating stare, she could tell it would be difficult to get a feel for him. He probably had a lot of practice at guarding his reactions.

The senator sipped his tea, never changing his gaze. "Oh, she's out shopping for the ball tonight—another excuse to make a big to do. These New Orleans' parties sure do get out of hand. Are you from New Orleans, Miss Cross?"

Samantha felt a trickle of fear run down her back. "No, I'm from Phoenix." The lie seemed reasonable enough to pass if Kevin didn't give her away. She took a long drink of tea, crossing her fingers that the current conversation would change course.

"The reason we wanted to drop by is to find out about Nathan Duvall." Kevin placed his hand on the back of Samantha's neck and began to gently make circular motions with his thumb.

She heard the senator admit to knowing Mr. Duvall, but unfortunately he was out of the country. Kevin's touch relaxed her, and she began to study the room in more detail. Photos along the walls appeared to be generations of family members: grandparents with painted rosy cheeks, moms and dads with their kids (who were probably the senator and his cousins, judging by the style of clothing), children grouped together at family outings. Samantha's eyes moved along the mantle of the fireplace and over to an end table. Her stomach tightened. Unconsciously, she stopped breathing. There on the table lay a deck of cards spread out like a clock—the same way her brother, Sam, had always laid his cards out. He had made up his own version of solitaire, placing kings where the three, six, nine and twelve should be on a clock and working the cards around the circle, queen through ace.

She refused to look at the senator. She could feel his gaze scrutinize her.

"Nathan doesn't have a residence in New Orleans. He only comes to attend certain social occasions."

Samantha couldn't stay focused on the conversation. A desperate need to leave the house spread through her. Calm down. Calm down. It's only a deck of cards. She took a deep breath, resuming her study of the room. More pictures hung on a wall near the window. This time a variety of individuals posed with the senator at different occasions. A man with blondish white hair standing next to the senator caught her eye. He had his arm around the senator, posing for the picture—the way he tilted his chin, his height and build. How many school pictures had Sam taken with his chin sticking out at that exact same angle? Perhaps, her imagination had gone rampant if only she could get a little closer to the picture.

"Something grab your attention, Miss Cross?" the senator asked.

Samantha tried to act casual, but everything seemed to be closing in on her. She self-consciously wiped her wet palm on her grey slacks. Sam couldn't be alive. It probably wasn't Sam in the picture. Who played cards in the house? She wanted to ask a million questions, but it seemed difficult to catch her breath. Her heart pounded, and a shooting pain hit the right side of her chest. Samantha turned to Kevin. "I have to get out of here."

Kevin took her elbow, helping her stand. His brow furrowed as his eyes searched her face.

"If Miss Cross would like, there are plenty of spare rooms upstairs?"

"I'm sure fresh air will work wonders," Kevin said, guiding Samantha towards the front door.

The hallway seemed long this time. Faces leered out of the pictures, which covered both sides of the hall. Samantha turned the gold knob on the large door. The knob turned easily in her hand, but nothing happened. She yanked on the door with an increasing surge of anxiety. The door flew open, and she stepped quickly out onto the porch. She felt the air pour back into her lungs, and her head started to clear.

"You know Maggie had a similar experience when she was pregnant with our first born," the senator said. He patted Samantha on the back. "I hope you feel better soon."

Samantha looked at Kevin, rolling her eyes skyward.

"Thanks for your time, Senator McCullen. I'll be in touch with you soon," Kevin said, shaking his hand.

James opened the car door, and Samantha slid in, feeling a shaky sense of relief to be getting away from the senator and his house.

"Are you all right?" Kevin asked, putting a hand on her shoulder as soon as the car door had shut.

Samantha felt her cheeks turn red. As a bodyguard, she should be fired. "I … I," she stuttered. Samantha took a deep breath. "I thought I saw a picture of my brother on the wall. The Senator seemed so strange to me. Do you think he was hiding something from us?"

"I know you didn't want to come to New Orleans." Kevin took her hand in his, straightening her fingers out, so they no longer made a fist. "Isn't this where your brother was killed?"

Samantha nodded, not trusting her voice. All this time she had kept her emotions in check. A small moan came from deep within her, and then tears began to slide down her cheeks. She tried catching her breath to keep herself calm, but everything inside her wanted out. She didn't want to cry in front of Kevin. She didn't want to cry at all. Samantha held her breath, keeping her eyes locked on the back of James's seat. She sucked in small amounts of air, but deep sobs began to escape from her chest.

He stroked her hair slowly and wiped away the tears that streaked down her face. "Have you had a chance to visit his grave?"

She shook her head from side to side. "No," she hiccupped, laying her head on his shoulder. Somehow, being next to Kevin made her feel better. Her breathing became steadier as he stroked her hair.

"There are quite a few cemeteries. We'll make some inquiries. The senator said Nathan Duvall shut down his New Orleans' office and took off for Brazil. So, I guess we're at a dead end for now. We can spend the night and find your brother's grave." Kevin reached across her and pulled her even closer into a bear hug.

Samantha nodded with her head pressed tightly to his chest. The smell of him felt almost as good as the sunshine that came in through the window and warmed her back. Her breathing began to return to normal with only an occasional hiccup to remind her of how ludicrous she felt. By the time the car stopped, Samantha had regained control of herself, and her cheeks had dried. She looked up to find they were parked outside a two-story, brick building with an arched entry. James got out of the car, unlocked the wrought iron gate that allowed access into the courtyard, and then briskly opened the car door for her.

There always seemed to be a distinct odor in the French Quarter near Bourbon Street—a smell of liquor either pissed or poured into the sewers that ran along the sidewalks. The smell reminded her of Eddie, and she gave an involuntary shudder. Perhaps, being in New Orleans did bring out the ghosts for her—a vision of his wide green eyes staring upward as he was rolled into a large plastic sheet popped into her head. That day she hadn't been fast enough to save Eddie—or Sam. Longing for her quiet house in Phoenix where she could pull the covers up over her head and make these terrible memories go away, she unconsciously tucked her hand underneath her jacket. The feel of the cool metal against her fingers reminded her of what she was here to do.

Sago palms, fan palms and elephant's ears nestled beneath deciduous trees. Even queen's wreath climbed up the trees, but the eye stopper was a tree right in the middle of the garden with the most beautiful red blossoms, that had scattered all over the star jasmine underneath it. The whole courtyard was covered in red brick from the walkways laid out between the deep seas of green plants to the four walls of the building, which surrounded the secret garden. A vine with pink flowers tried to creep up and cover the stairs leading to a second story.

"James lives on the top floor; we've got the bottom," Kevin said, opening a plain white door and waiting for her to enter.

Inside Samantha stood rooted in place. The living room was completely done in red from the walls to the floral printed rug. The furniture took turns alternating between solid red and a floral pattern. Picture frames were trimmed with gold along with the large mirror that sat above the white fireplace. "Is this your place?" Samantha asked as her eyes darted from one floral print to another.

Kevin chuckled. "It is, but the previous owner did all the decorating. I planned on changing everything, but my mom loved it. So, I left it alone. You relax for a minute. I'm going to make sure our food is ready."

"Food?" Samantha's stomach growled at just the mention of food. "Not so fast." Jerking her gun out of her holster, she walked through the living room and into a small hall. Another entryway led into the kitchen where an aroma of garlic escaped out of a large bag sitting on the counter. Through the kitchen and around the corner, she moved stealthily into the dining room, which opened back into the hall.

Kevin stood at the entrance waiting for her along with James, who had brought in their bags. "If they were hiding in the bedroom, I'd probably be dead by now."

Samantha rolled her eyes. She crept towards the bedroom, ignoring the fact that she looked ridiculous and that Kevin refused to wipe the smirk off of his face. The bedroom, closet, and bathroom were all completely empty of murderers, except for her, of course. Lowering the gun, her blue eyes locked with her reflection. She snorted at herself. Contempt wouldn't keep her or Kevin alive.

She trudged out of the bathroom and into the living room, slumping down on the red sofa. James had left, and she could hear Kevin removing containers from the bag in the kitchen. Picking up a red pillow, she idly traced her finger along the brocade. Her head still reeled from the memories of Sam and Eddie. She couldn't help wanting to visit her brother's grave, getting rid of her brother's killer hadn't given her any closure after all—only more emptiness.

At least, the pictures that decorated the walls were paintings of Vieux Carre', and not pictures she imagined to be of her brother. She could call Lisa and tell her she was here. Lisa, her brother's girlfriend at the time he was killed, had told her that Sam had been buried in an unmarked grave. Maybe Lisa even knew where the grave was, but the last time they had spoken Lisa lied and told Samantha that Ani Goro was here in New Orleans. It had definitely been a ploy to get her back to New Orleans, but why?

"Dinner's ready."

And why precisely did she care about Lisa when she could be staring at the most beautiful man she had ever seen? With his jacket off and his white shirt sleeves rolled up, everything else seemed to drift away.

She got up off the couch and walked towards him as he leaned against the doorway. His hands reached out, and he pulled her hips close to his. Then he kissed her until she felt her world tilt. As her body melted into his, part of her mind decided that the floral printed rug would most likely be soft enough if they couldn't make it to the bedroom.

Kevin pulled away. His breathing was heavy, and his eyes had taken on an intense hunger. "I'd lock you in and throw away the key, but I found something interesting in my mail."

Damn, maybe he could throw away the key for a little while. She let him pull her along to the dining room. This room paled in comparison to the living room, or more accurately the parlor. One wall was brick, and the other three walls were painted plain white. French doors opened to the backyard, which sported hibiscus and cape plumbago shrubs.

"I love your gardens. When I lived here, I would spend time walking around the city, trying to learn as much about the plants as I could. Well, the history of New Orleans, too." Her plate had already been filled with chicken gumbo, vegetable medley and something she wasn't quite sure what it was, but it looked good. A white envelope with gold calligraphy sat right beside her plate.

"Take a look at that," Kevin said, sitting down and pushing the envelope closer to her with his fingertips.

The envelope was addressed to Kevin Jacobs and contained an invitation to a New Year's Eve Ball. "Is this the one Senator McCullen talked about?"

"Exactly, I have a feeling about this Nathan Duvall, and you don't seem real keen on the senator—although he's always been good to me in the past. So, what do you think?"

"I guess that's reasonable. Can we get clothes for a ball in a couple of hours?"

"Better than that—we can have them delivered. Laissez les bon temps rouler! Let the good times roll."

Samantha looked down at her plate of food. This really was a lot like an emotional roller coaster.

"Try the fried eggplant. It's covered in a shrimp and crab sauce. It's my absolute favorite."

Samantha took a bite and savored every succulent flavor. It was a cream sauce, but there was no denying it had a bit of kick in it. Her eyes wandered around the dining room, taking in the dark wood floors and the large beams running across the wood-planked ceiling. She caught Kevin watching her and couldn't help but notice how perfectly defined his lips were. What would it be like if she let him kiss her anywhere he wanted to?

Chapter Seven

Silver sequins glittered and shimmered, casting light in every direction. If she were to pick out a dress for New Year's Eve, this would be it. She simply hadn't realized this was New Year's Eve. The days seemed jumbled as if she had missed one somewhere. And nobody had said it was New Year's Eve though apparently it was. Of course, considering she had spent Christmas Day getting her head slammed into concrete in a warehouse in Juarez, maybe a person could even misplace a week and not know where it went.

Strapless but tight enough across the bosom that it even made her look busty, and then below the hips the dress switched from sequins to shimmering soft silk strips, which floated, making her feel way sexier than she ever had in her life. This dress even beat out the red strappy number she had picked up in Juarez (same trip as the head slamming, except the shopping had come first). Tucking her bobbed blonde hair behind her ear, Samantha grinned and showed off big red lips. She had paid special attention to the makeup (especially the lips)—smoke grey eye shadow to make her blue eyes pop and big red lips to make Kevin think of anything naughty that he wanted to.

What had gotten into her? What happened to the whole keeping him at bay thing? Samantha knew. It was the constant touching. Nothing over the top, but still it was desensitizing her. Would his hands touch her neck or the small of her back? Would he sit too close, making her pulse race? And while all these thoughts bounced around in her head, she caught his reflection in the mirror.

He came up behind her dressed in a tux, which not surprisingly didn't look too terribly different from what he usually wore. The difference was the way her body reacted to him. She didn't pull away anymore; in fact despite herself she leaned into him. Everything about her wanted him to touch her, and that's when she realized just how functional the dress really was.

She felt his hands slide into the layered strips of silk that made up the bottom half of her dress. Her head tipped backwards and her eyes closed as he ran his fingers up her legs until they traced along her thong. Her breath caught, as his fingers teased her.

"You look amazing," he whispered.

She almost whimpered; she wanted him so bad.

"Don't worry, I'll have you home shortly after midnight," he said, giving her a crooked smile as he removed his hands from her. He very gently straightened her skirt, and then with a devilish grin, he put his finger in his mouth and sucked it.

Samantha just looked at him. What could she say? Her body hadn't stopped trembling. She hoped tonight would be a short one. Couldn't they ring in the New Year doing some position that wasn't always legal? Well, depending on the state.

"Kevin," she said, putting a hand on his shoulder to stop him before he got completely out of the bathroom. "What about my gun?"

"You can take it in the car."

"O.K., but what about at the party?"

"You don't need it."

"I could take my knife."

He gave her a cocky grin. "The only hole you have that the knife will fit in is mine. And I'm not sharing." He picked her up and swung her into the bedroom. "Don't worry. We'll do a little shakedown at the party, and I'll have you back here, naked across that bed, before you can say, 'damn, I wish I had brought my gun.'"

Samantha huffed as he put her down. "The last time I went out without my gun, I almost got shot to death in a hot tub."

"It was the company you were keeping. Everyone knows Jack is as dangerous as they come. Mr. Thompson wanted you with him to see if it would keep him in line a little." Kevin took her hand, pulling her towards the bedroom door.

Samantha snagged her gun off the dresser and stopped to toss her jacket over the top of it. She was damn sure taking it in the car.

Kevin held the front door open for her as she made her way into the dimly lit courtyard. She scanned the garden area and even the rooftops, stepping carefully out from under the balcony. The upstairs landing was empty, and Samantha suppressed a shiver. Gaslights lit up the walkway, and a delicate orange perfume floated in the breeze, giving the night air the sweet smell of enchantment.

James waited patiently, smiling as he held the door to the limo open.

"I like the ride," Samantha said as she slid in grateful that her new heels didn't make walking a nightmare. She had always been more comfortable in tennis shoes.

"I'm more interested in the ride home." Kevin ran his fingers along her bare shoulder.

Her stomach did a quick free-for-all before she turned towards the window in hopes of keeping the warm feeling that was spreading through her at bay. Christmas lights hung across the streets, making New Orleans appear to be a winter wonderland with no snow. She wondered what her brother would have thought if he could see her now: looking like a movie star, riding in a limo to a New Year's party hosted by a senator, and packing a .45, which was tucked under her grey silk jacket. He'd probably laugh and say well done.

Kevin took her hand and kissed it with his lips. "When this is all over, I promise never to bring you back here."

She squeezed his hand as James stopped the limo in front of a large hotel. The valet ran over to open the door for them. Samantha carefully placed her gun and jacket in the seat, before stepping out of the car. The gun wasn't as hard to leave behind as she had thought especially with Kevin's hand touching her waist. He guided her into the foyer and then into a maze of small rooms where men sat smoking cigars and women laughed while sipping champagne. A blues melody rippled through the air, making conversation possible but at the same time impossible to eavesdrop. Kevin would stop occasionally to shake someone's hand and to introduce Samantha as they plucked their way from the smaller rooms to the open ballroom.

The lights from the large chandeliers cascaded around the room and descended on her until she felt like a jewel, sparkling in the mist of a New Year. Kevin wrapped his arm around her waist and caught her up into a slow dance. This party could definitely make her top five list.

Senator McCullen stood out in his white tux, talking with a couple that looked like they had only recently returned from the Bahamas, or a few too many sessions at the tanning salon. He caught Samantha watching him and nodded, but from that moment on, she could tell his gaze never left her. Maybe her approach had not been direct enough this afternoon. She could ask him if he knew her brother. And that would be the end of it, or the start of it. Her fingers itched to wrap themselves around the cold butt of her gun. Ignoring the need for her newfound security blanket, she drove the sound of her racing heart out of her head.

Senator McCullen never made a false move though. He chatted with one group and then moved on to next. Dancing around the ballroom wasn't a bad way to keep her eye on him, and she noticed instantly when his face paled and he took on a rigid stance.

"Turn me the other way," Samantha whispered urgently in Kevin's ear. He spun her around, so she could see in the opposite direction. It felt like a fist hit her in the stomach. It was Lisa. Samantha jerked Kevin's arm hard and started off the dance floor after her.

Lisa tensed, her eyes flew open wide, and then her face broke into a smile. She threw her arms open to embrace Samantha. "Oh, Karen, I can't believe I found you and here of all places." Lisa pulled her into a hug.

Samantha patted Lisa's back—half of her flooded with relief while the other half struggled with thoughts of betrayal. She had longed to be with Lisa after Sam had died, but now she didn't know if she could trust her. Removing herself from the embrace, she squeezed Lisa's hands to not seem overly rude. The first thing that struck her was that Lisa didn't appear to be a grieving girlfriend. She looked like a belle of the ball. Her ash blond hair swooped to the side and glittered with tiny blue jewels that matched her tight fitting dress. What stood out the most was the diamond necklace and the, at least, three karat diamond ring that sparkled on her left hand.

Samantha took a step backwards as if she had been slapped. Barely two weeks had passed since her brother had been shot to death, and Lisa was already engaged.

Lisa twisted the ring self-consciously. "I borrowed the jewelry," she whispered.

Samantha felt her head spinning in a thousand different directions—mad not mad, forgiving not forgiving. She fought to stay in control of her emotions. No point in repeating another episode like the one at the senator's house. She took a deep breath. "Lisa, this is Kevin Jacobs. Kevin, this is Lisa, my brother's girlfriend." The words were out, and she couldn't take them back. She bit her lip, ignoring the blunder.

Lisa didn't blink. She trudged up a tight smile that didn't make it all the way to her eyes. "I know Mr. Jacobs. He used to come to Mr. Guerrero's often."

Samantha felt a flash of anger roar through her. Of course, Lisa would know Kevin; she worked for the Guerrero family. She was the one that had introduced Sam to Ani Goro in the first place.

"Lisa, why don't we meet in the morning for coffee, and you could take us to Karen's brother's grave." Kevin's fingers tightened around Samantha's waist.

Lisa paused and slowly nodded her head. "We could do Leno's at nine? You look great, Karen. You really do." She squeezed Samantha's shoulder. "I was so worried about you."

"In the morning then," Kevin said as he turned Samantha back to the dance floor and held her to him while they circled around the floor. She unclenched her fists and jaw as a feeling of security washed over her. He had pulled her away from the tidal wave of emotion that had threatened to rip her apart, and he hadn't even given away her false identity. She snuggled into his chest, knowing if she didn't have the strength for all the emotional crap that he did. She'd deal with Lisa tomorrow.

They moved slowly around the dance floor, so Samantha could watch the senator and Lisa. But neither of them stayed with any group for too long, nor did they make any sudden moves.

As the dance ended, they came to a stop near the senator. "I suppose you haven't heard from Nathan Duvall?" Kevin asked.

Senator McCullen pumped Kevin's hand with a long handshake. "I do believe he is out of the country, but if he shows up, I'll make sure you're the first to know. And Miss Cross, I do hope you are feeling better."

"Much," Samantha said.

"Then I would be obliged if you would be so kind as to dance with me?" He held his hand out and with a slight bow waited for Samantha to accept.

Samantha glanced at Kevin.

"I'll get us something to drink," he said as he slipped away towards the corner of the room where a waiter stood behind a bar.

Samantha took Senator McCullen's hand, and he eased her out onto the dance floor. They began a slow waltz which made Samantha slightly relieved since she really wasn't a good dancer.

"I really hate to bring this up, but I'm wondering if Samantha Cross is your real name?"

Samantha lost her step, and the Senator had to steady her.

"I'm sorry, Senator McCullen, I'm completely knocked off balance by that. Why would you ask that?"

"Oh, don't let me throw you off dear. It's simply that you remind me so much of someone I know."

Samantha's heart leaped out of her chest, and she hoped the senator hadn't realized how sweaty her palms were. "Do you mind telling me who that might be?"

A man tapped the senator's shoulder, and a brunette with soft flowing curls and bright red lipstick squealed with delight. "Senator McCullen, oh, I must cut in. It's been so long since I've seen you."

Samantha found herself dancing with the brunette's date. To her annoyance, he quickly spun her away from the senator.

"Sorry to have interrupted. Charlotte absolutely adores the senator. My name is Ruben and yours is?"

"I hope you don't mind, Ruben, but my date is waiting for me." Samantha slipped off the dance floor and met Kevin coming back from the bar. She leaned in, taking her drink from him. "The senator wants to know what my real name is, and he thinks I look like someone he knows."

"Who?"

"I don't know. We got interrupted by that bimbo that's dancing with him."

"We'll find out soon enough." Kevin put his hand on her neck and began to gently trace circles. "By the way that's a sazerac."

Samantha fought the urge to cut back in on the dance, but the music was ending. She took a sip of her drink, shook her head and looked at Kevin for an explanation."

"I told you. It's a sazerac."

Samantha took another sip, slower this time; it was sweet and sour and tasted like licorice. Her fingers tightened around her old-fashioned glass as the senator left the dance floor. Samantha watched in horror as the brunette led him into another room.

"Kevin," Samantha said, nudging him with her elbow, "we should go after him."

Kevin guided her through the now drunken crowd towards the door the senator had gone through. Samantha bumped into a guy, who avoided dumping a drink down her dress by jerking the drink away and letting it spill on the floor. "Excuse me," she mumbled as she went around him, barely keeping her own drink from sloshing. Shoving her way into a small parlor, she found it stuffed full of people taking a smoke break. Frantically, she scanned the sofas and settees but didn't spot the senator. The next room offered a long buffet table and lots of partiers filling their plates. One more door and she found herself back at the lobby to the hotel.

"Did you see which way Senator McCullen went?" Kevin asked the bellhop, who was standing next to the glass door.

"Oh, he left." The young man bobbed up and down, showing a mouth full of braces.

"We need to go," Kevin whispered urgently. He handed their glasses to the bellhop, wrapped his arm around her waist and ushered her out the door before anyone could open it for them.

"What is it?" She craned her head around, trying to figure out what the problem was. A few of the partiers had filtered out, but no one she recognized. A tall, lean man watched them leave, but then he waved to someone down the hall and went back into the party.

"Time to get you home."

Anger and disappointment bubbled inside of her. Why couldn't she have had two more minutes with the senator? "Let's go. I guess," Samantha said, as she blew out a big sigh. What a crappy night. Lisa was such a fraud—already engaged. Maybe Lisa had helped Ani Goro set her brother up.

A cold wind whipped around them as they stepped outside. Samantha couldn't help but shake as they waited for the limo to be brought around. She snuggled up to Kevin as he draped his tux jacket around her. More than caring about warmth, an urge to have her gun gnawed at her gut; she felt like a sitting target with the light of the lobby behind her and the dark night in front of her.

Kevin's limo pulled up, and a valet attendant politely opened the door for them.

Samantha slid into the car and clutched her gun to her. As they pulled away from the lights, she took the clip out and checked to make sure all of her bullets were in place. Glancing at Kevin, she met his gaze as he studied her.

"Normally, girls don't try to kill me until the breakup period of our relationship."

"I wanted to get a head start, considering I'm a quick study."

Kevin pulled her into his arms. "I know you're scared. So, now that you've killed Ani, do you think you could stop running around being a hitman?"

Samantha twisted in his arms to face him. "I thought since I saved your life you would quit with the lectures."

"I backed off for two days," he said as he began to kiss her neck.

Samantha groaned. This is what made Kevin so dangerous—the ability for him to rock her emotions in less than two seconds. "Kevin," she muttered, but he took the opportunity to softly bite her lip. She felt his hands shift to her waist, drawing her closer as he kissed her full on. The fierceness and possession demanded her attention as his hands slipped inside her dress and softly stroked her hips. Every part of her burned, and she felt shaky when the car came to a stop.

Samantha caught her breath and adjusted her dress as James got out of the car and opened the door for her. She carefully arranged the gun so her jacket hung over it, but wouldn't hinder her ability to fire. As soon as she stood on the sidewalk, she felt Kevin's hands wrap around her waist, keeping her body close to his. Lampposts lit the street, offering shadowy light between pools of darkness. James unlocked the gate, making a loud squeaking noise as he pushed it open.

While Kevin held her tightly to him, she felt silly holding her gun and trying to remain vigilant. The hair on the back of her neck stood up, but she couldn't tell if something was wrong or just a reaction to Kevin breathing on her. Entering the courtyard, Kevin slipped in front of her in order to unlock the house door. A sigh as soft as a slight breeze caused Samantha to spin around, keeping Kevin between the door and her. And there he was— perfectly still. His blonde hair gleamed in the dim light. Most of his body remained concealed in shadow, but the shape of his face and the color of his hair left no doubt in her mind. Everything in her froze—her mind, her fingers, even her breath seemed to be caught in her throat. The back gate he was standing beside moved ever so slightly, and he was gone.

Kevin opened the door to the house and pulled her inside, kicking the door closed behind them. He took the gun from her, laying it on the couch.

"You didn't see him did you?"

"See who?" he asked as he began to nibble on her ear.

She opened her mouth, but the only thing that came out was a shocked, "Oh."

Kevin scooped her up and carried her into the bedroom.

Her head spun—half of her thinking about her brother and the other half feeling kisses trail from her collarbone down along the scalloped edge of her dress until he reached the teardrop center of the bodice.

She started to push him away and tell him about Sam when she felt her dress slide all the way to the floor.

Chapter Eight

Sunshine splashed in on the white brick walls, making everything feel light and effortless. Samantha watched the light pool on his brown curly hair. She didn't dare move. Yesterday she had wondered what his abs would feel like against her body; today she knew exactly how that felt. She shivered thinking about the night before. It was almost intoxicating.

He rolled over, dragging her to him. His dark blue eyes locked with hers as his hands began to trail over her skin.

The ringing of a cell phone cut through the silence. Kevin's jaw tightened, before reaching over her and grabbing the phone. "What?" He threw his head back and groaned. "Fine," he said, clicking off the cell phone and tossing it on the bed. "That was your girlfriend, Lisa. She wants to meet at eight instead of nine."

"She is not my girlfriend. Did you see the rock she flaunted last night? My brother…." Her voice trailed off as she remembered the man standing in the shadows last night. It had been Sam hadn't it? Had she seen him holding a gun?

"Don't get too panicked. We'll meet her. See what she has to say, and go from there. Samantha," he whispered, brushing her jaw with his thumb and bringing her gaze back to him. "I can't lose you. So, when this is wrapped up with your brother, I'm making sure you never work as a hitman again."

How many ways could her emotions be pulled? If she had given herself any time to think about her and Kevin, she would've known this was coming.

"What was your brother's name?"

Samantha stared at him. "Sam, Sam Cane." The name felt heavy on her tongue as if attached to it was a lot of responsibility.

Kevin stiffened then looked out the window. "I've got a friend in the police department here. I'll have him check into it to make sure Lisa's story is on the up and up." He gave her a quick kiss on the cheek, before he rolled out of the bed and went into the bathroom.

The click of the bathroom door sounded so final in the quiet bedroom. Did Kevin know Sam? New Orleans gave her a headache. Senator McCullen, Lisa, and now Kevin were all hiding something, or did it even matter because Sam was still alive—maybe. Or was she imagining every little movement and shadow to be a conspiracy. What would Jack say? Maybe she relied a little too much on what Jack would say.

Pushing herself out of bed, she walked around the end of it, feeling goose bumps on her arms. The transparent yellow curtains swayed slightly from the breeze of the large open bedroom windows. She hadn't even noticed they were open last night. She certainly hadn't gotten cold.

Her dress lay by the foot of the bed, and she picked it up, feeling the color rise in her cheeks as she remembered how it got there. O.K., a few things in New Orleans were outstanding. Hanging her dress in the closet, she found a man's robe and wrapped it around herself. A small smirk appeared on her face as she inspected his closet. All the clothes in Kevin's closet were men's: black, grey and brown suits; lots of white dress shirts; a couple of striped cotton shirts next to some jeans. At least, no reminders of Becki hung in the closet.

Her bare feet padded over the wood floors as she fetched her gun out of the living room. What if Sam really was alive? What was she supposed to do now? The whole point had been to kill to Ani and then find out who ordered the hit on Sam. It would have been helpful to have gotten that information from Ani, but could she have believed him?

As she entered the bedroom, Kevin stepped out of the bathroom with a towel wrapped around his waist. "I don't mind making Lisa wait," he said, grinning and tilting his head towards the bed.

"Did you know Sam?" She stared him straight in the eye, not even realizing she had her .45 clutched in her hand.

"No." Kevin crossed his arms over his chest.

"Do you know who ordered the hit on Sam?"

Kevin dropped his gaze and walked around her. "We're going to find out. I'll get dressed, you shower."

He was lying. She knew it. Her stomach clenched and her head pounded. This emotional crap riddled her with loss. She wanted out of New Orleans. Why did everything turn to crap when she came here? Tossing her gun down on the bed, she slammed the door to the bathroom. Fine, everyone can lie, but she would figure this out.

Showering as quickly as possible, Samantha toweled off and pulled on her suit. She could face Lisa. No problem. Slipping into her holster and tucking her knife in her boot, she began to feel more confident. Why let any of it drag her down? Lisa would probably lie like Kevin, and she couldn't take it out on either one of them if Sam was still alive.

She stepped into the bedroom and a whiff of coffee and smoke caught her attention. Moving into the hall, she poked her head around the corner. Kevin was smashing a cigarillo out and talking on the phone.

"I do think that's best. I'm not worried about myself. If I stay on the move, no one will know where I'm going anyway. O.K., I'll send her back with James."

Samantha didn't move. She closed her eyes, fighting the wave of nausea that rolled through her. No big deal. She was ready to get the hell out of here. She backtracked into the bedroom, grabbed her gun off of the bed, and stuffed it into the holster underneath her jacket. Quickly tossing the rest of her things into the brown shopping bag, she ignored Kevin as he came into the bedroom and blocked the doorway.

"I talked with Brody."

"I heard you," she snapped, picking up her bag.

"Samantha..." He stepped forward, closing the distance between them.

"No, let's get this meeting with Lisa over with, so I can have James get me the hell out of here."

Kevin grabbed a hold of her, gripping her arms and pulling her to him. "I'm going to get this stuff straightened out, and when I do, we're taking off together."

"Sure, sounds good. Now could you let go of me?"

Kevin dropped her arms and backed off. His cheeks were red, and his eyes were lowered under thick lashes. "You'll see."

"I see someone who can't level with me, but I should be used to that by now."

Neither of them moved—anger rolled off both of them. The flutter of the curtain caught her eye and dragged her attention to the window. The gunman wore a black ski mask and stood completely still.

Samantha lurched forward, knocking Kevin to the floor. Glass and wood sprayed the bedroom as they fell into the hall. Drawing her gun, she crouched in the hall and waited to hear something. The curtains continued to flutter, and every once in a while, a bird chirped. After a minute of remaining perfectly still while anticipating someone charging into the house or more bullets cascading through the air, she stood up slowly on now aching legs. Very cautiously, Samantha entered the bedroom, daring to peek outside. The backyard was completely empty.

Kevin stood frozen his eyes never leaving her. His features were drawn as tight as his clenched fists.

Samantha stared at him glad that he didn't carry a gun. Some people didn't have the control, and she sensed Kevin was definitely one of them. "He's gone."

"Did you get a look at him?"

Samantha shook her head. "A guy with a muscular build and a black ski mask."

Kevin pulled his phone out of his pocket. "James we're ready to go. Come get our bags, and keep your eyes open. Someone shot out the windows in the bedroom." He clicked off his phone and threw his arm around Samantha's waist to stop her from getting by him.

"Thanks," he whispered.

"Sure." Samantha pushed past him and went into the living room to check the front windows.

The locks on the door started jiggling as James tumbled in, holding his gun and looking like he might be having trouble breathing. Perspiration stood out on his forehead, making his receding hairline even more noticeable.

Kevin smirked. "Relax, James. That's why we have Samantha. Grab our bags."

James tugged on his collar as if to loosen it a bit. He looked around the living room with wild eyes, shrugged, and plodded to the bedroom.

Samantha kept her gun out. She moved past Kevin, making sure not to touch him. If he wanted to keep things from her then fine, she would try to make sure he lived long enough to tell her the truth.

Once outside the door, she stepped out from under the balcony and spun around, checking out the roofline—nothing but blue sky and a few white clouds floating lazily about. Surveying the entire courtyard, she waited. A bead of sweat rolled off her forehead. It wasn't particularly warm, and part of her felt a little shaky. This really was a tough business. The hardest part seemed to be keeping herself from splintering into a thousand pieces.

"I had to turn off the coffee pot and stove," Kevin said as he came out the door. His eyes remained weary as he scanned the garden area. The tightness around his eyes and mouth made him appear older.

Samantha stayed in front of him and led the way to the Mercedes. She stalled at the unlocked gate, scanning the street for anyone out of place. A motorcycle drove by, and across the street, a group of middle-aged women admired the display window of the pastry shop for pets. She put her gun down by her side and strode quickly to the parked car, jerking the door open for Kevin to get in.

Kevin got into the backseat as James shoved every-thing in the front seat and jumped in, starting the car with one quick motion.

Samantha stepped in, slammed the door and slumped into the seat. "You could put your head down."

Kevin's mouth fell open. "You must love me deep down."

"You lie, but it's my job to keep you alive."

Kevin's hand found its way to the back of her neck and stroked it. "You could always shoot me, if you didn't want me touching you."

Oh, this was bad. She felt everything inside her tilt upside down as her breath came out in a small involuntary gasp. "Stop touching me or I might."

Kevin slid closer and wrapped his arm around her. He kissed her ear and whispered, "This will work out. I can feel it."

Samantha leaned away from him, ignoring how much she wanted to crumple in his arms. He was a liar, but she didn't think she wanted him shot down in front of her or ever.

The car stopped and Samantha took a deep breath. She holstered her gun and opened the door. Stepping onto the sidewalk, she cautiously scanned the area. Cars lined the street, and people were packed into the tiny outdoor cafe. The wind had picked up, and the smell of fresh baked bread swirled in the air, reminding her she hadn't eaten.

Lisa stood in the open archway, holding a cup of coffee. She waived and walked over to meet them. "Do you guys want to get breakfast or a Beignet?"

"No," Samantha snapped, noticing the engagement ring was missing from her hand.

Lisa frowned. "I told you I borrowed that jewelry."

Samantha shrugged. "Do you know where they buried my brother?"

Lisa met Samantha's scrutiny with steady brown eyes. "Sure. The cemetery is across the street."

Samantha turned her head in the direction Lisa pointed. Sure enough, surrounded by a black wrought iron fence lay a cement garden decorated with crosses, angels and headstones. Samantha followed Lisa, dissecting every-thing from her neatly styled, ash-blond hair that hit below her shoulder to her dark blue, sling back heels. The blue plaid jacket and skirt looked a lot more expensive than Lisa's old wardrobe.

Her stomach clenched as they entered the cemetery. She felt Kevin's hand slide under her jacket and rest at the small of her back. They wove their way through the city of the dead by walkways made of vaults that lined each side of the path. Family names jumped out from large headstones, listing loved ones that had been buried together. For the families that could afford being buried in style, crypts that resembled small houses were surrounded by their own private wrought iron fences.

Samantha remembered the grassy cemetery her mother was buried at in Florida. The grass seemed so much more calming compared to the rows of cement that kept the bodies from floating out of the ground when the water level got too high.

They finally came to a stop at the back of the cemetery, and a large block of cement protruded up with a very long list of names engraved on the stone wall behind it. Saman-tha scanned the list, finding her brother's name towards the bottom. She froze. Her heart pounded in her head as she read the name *Samuel Tyler Cane*. Flashing lights exploded in her head, her body swayed and she blinked rapidly.

"I know it's not a proper burial.... But after the fire there wasn't much left," Lisa said as her voice trailed off.

"Why did you lie to me about Ani Goro?" Samantha ground out the words as she reached inside her jacket and gripped her gun with shaking fingers.

Lisa's eyes widened. "Karen, I wanted you to come back. I thought if I told you he was here you would come back."

"But, you knew he was in Phoenix?"

"No." Lisa tucked her long hair behind her ears to keep the wind from whipping it around. Her eyes fell on Samantha's jacket. "Why are you carrying a gun?"

Samantha laughed. Lisa looked as perfectly angelic as the stone angel they had passed on the way in. The only real similarity was that they were both made of stone. "Because Ani gunned my brother down in front of me, and now I protect myself."

"Karen, I want you to move in with me, and we'll work this out together—you and I."

"No, Lisa. I don't want to work things out." She wrenched her hand away from the gun and took off in the direction they had come, crisscrossing from one path to the next. She felt disgusted and betrayed by everyone. Shooting Lisa wouldn't get her the answers she wanted;

98

besides there were too many tourists. Someone would notice. Then she would be in a cell; instead of putting the pieces of her life back together.

Kevin's footsteps echoed behind her, trying to keep pace with her, but she had to keep moving. The need to get away from the cement vaults and the looming crosses had become overwhelming. Had she really seen Sam the night before? It had been dark, but he hadn't been completely in the shadows. Why would he come there and not talk to her? The thought of her brother cremated and dumped into a city vault made her skin crawl. She ran out of the wrought iron gate and across the street, barely missing an oncoming car. The jerks never slowed down; they thought they owned the streets. She jumped in the car and slammed the door behind her.

James didn't move. As her breathing steadied and the pounding in her head subsided, Samantha listened to the overpowering silence. A trickle of perspiration ran down her back, and she shook her head in an attempt to figure out what the hell was wrong with this day. A strange smell lingered in the car, and instead of feeling better, Samantha started to feel worse. She looked into the rearview mirror and realized James still hadn't moved. His head leaned to the side, and his mouth hung open. The smell of gunpowder caught her attention and panic started to course through her.

Kevin appeared outside the driver's side window—his jaw set and his eyes wide. He yanked open the back door and jerked her out.

She felt shaky like her knees would buckle any minute. Grabbing onto Kevin, she let his strong hands steady her. Everything around her moved too fast for her to focus. All the faces of the pedestrians blurred together—except one. He stood across the street, watching her as he casually leaned against a tan sedan. Wearing jeans and a light blue long sleeved shirt, the sun reflected off of his blonde hair as he stared directly at her. She took a couple of steps towards him when the sound of a car horn blared, and Kevin jerked her back to him.

"What the hell are you thinking?" he yelled at her as he hailed a cab. Opening the door, Kevin carefully pushed Samantha inside. "To the airport," he said to the cabby. Then he folded Samantha up into his arms, holding her tightly to him. "You're in shock," he whispered quietly into her ear.

She felt her body start to shake, but she couldn't get her mind to quit racing. Was her brother, Samuel Cane, really alive? Why after she had been through so much did everything come crumbling down on her like this? She breathed in his scent and somewhere in her mind she knew the answer was Kevin. She couldn't lose him. Not now, not ever.

He slid his black suit jacket off and wrapped it around her shoulders, while pulling her close to him. He gently stroked her hair as the miles ticked by along the freeway. Her heart started to slow down, and her eyes began to focus again. The buttons on his white cotton shirt were small and clear, and the side door to the cab had brown upholstery, which was well worn but clean. The floor of the cab was covered with dark mats placed carefully on top of clear plastic underneath. She raised her eyes to Kevin's face. His eyes no longer held the vulnerable look that sleep deprivation had given him in weeks past. In fact, his jaw was clenched, and his eyes held a sharp alertness despite his efforts to comfort her.

The cabby zipped into a slot at the first entrance to the airport. He swiveled around, looking at Kevin. "Is this good?"

Kevin nodded. "How much?"

"Twenty-two fifty. You guys have a good flight."

Kevin handed him some folded up bills. Then he opened the door and tugged Samantha out with him.

She felt relieved to find her legs didn't shake anymore. Standing up straight, she numbly handed his jacket back to him. They made their way into the terminal, getting in line at the ticket counter. Kevin kept her tucked underneath his arm until they reached the front of the line.

The petite blond behind the counter twitched her lips. "How may I help you?"

"One ticket to Phoenix and one to New York, departing as soon as possible."

She consulted her computer and tapped her nails on the keyboard while she waited. "The Phoenix flight leaves in thirty minutes. If you have bags, they won't have time to be loaded. There's another leaving in three hours."

"No, we'll take the first one. How about New York?"

"That one leaves in an hour," she said, showing her most practiced smile. "That will be $760.00 for both."

Kevin pulled out a large wad of money held together with a gold clip. He handed her eight one-hundred dollar bills and put the rest back in his pants pocket.

"I'll need to see IDs," she said as she marked the bills and held them up to the light.

Kevin tugged his wallet out as Samantha fumbled around in her jacket pocket. She didn't want to go back to Phoenix—not without Kevin. Grudgingly, she handed him her license. "Don't you think I should go with you?"

Taking her license, he shook his head and kissed her on top of the forehead. They got their tickets and started for the escalator.

Samantha jerked on his arm to get him to stop. "I think I should go with you."

Kevin squared off and faced her. "Brody needs you in Phoenix."

"No, he doesn't. I heard you this morning. It's your idea to send me back."

He took a deep breath and blew it out slowly. "I think this thing is rocking out of control, and I don't want you anywhere near it."

"That is complete crap. You know what it's like when I'm with Jack. It wasn't a week ago you didn't want me anywhere near him because he was too dangerous."

"I can't protect you, Samantha. If someone tries to shoot me and gets you in the crossfire, I can't deal with that."

Stomping off towards the escalator, Samantha almost collided with an elderly couple when Kevin yanked her back to him. His mouth was set in a tight line, and anger radiated off of him. "At least, Jack can protect you. He's one of the best gunmen I know. I can't even carry a gun."

Samantha waited; she refused to acknowledge that even part of what he said was true.

"I'm a convict, Samantha. If I'm caught with a gun, I go back in, and I'm not going back."

"That only means you need me even more."

He grabbed her hand in his, pulling her onto the escalator. "I'm not going to fight with you. Your plane is leaving. Stick with Jack or stick with Bruno, but Ken and

Allen don't know their asses from a hole in the ground. I will clear this up and soon."

At the top of the escalator, Kevin pulled her along until they stood outside the women's bathroom. He took his jacket off and handed it to her; then he leaned in and whispered in her ear, "Go in the stall, wrap your gun and holster in the jacket, and toss it in the trash."

Samantha stared at him. She hadn't even thought about it, but now from where she was standing, she could see the security check gate. She took the jacket with a deep loathing for herself. How could she expect Kevin to want her around when she kept falling apart and couldn't even think straight?

On stilted legs, she made her way into the bathroom. Her hands shook as she latched the stall door. Taking deep breaths, she forced her hands to quit trembling before she slipped her jacket off and began to pull off the holster. As an afterthought, she searched the ceiling to make sure there were no surveillance cameras. For once something seemed to be in her favor. She carefully wrapped the gun and holster in Kevin's jacket. Her hand reached for the lock when she remembered her knife. She sucked in air, kicking herself for being so stupid. Pulling the knife out, she couldn't help but think how mad Jack was going to be. No one came in or out of the bathroom, and she quickly walked to the exit, pushed the jacket into the swinging lid of the trash can and left.

Her heart broke when she saw Kevin leaning against the wall, waiting for her. What if this was the last time she saw him? At the moment, he looked like he could handle anything, but she had her doubts. He was running—she knew the feeling well. He clasped her hand in his, and Samantha welcomed the reassurance.

As they approached the security gate, her pulse sped up. The guards kept the crowd moving forward. Finally, it was her turn to go through the metal detector, nothing beeped and no one slammed her up against the counter for a frisk.

She slumped in a chair as Kevin checked the departure time.

He sat down next to her, not speaking as he stared out the large windows.

"How do you plan on protecting yourself if you don't carry a gun?" Samantha asked, tasting the acidic bile in her throat.

"I'm not going to let anyone know where I'm going. With Ani dead, I really thought I didn't have much to worry about. I planned on finding out about the laundry houses and calling it a wrap. But someone wants me dead real bad."

"Who do you think that is?"

"I think Lisa knows. She was long gone by the time we got back to the car."

"Flight 173 for Phoenix is now boarding. Anyone who needs assistance or is traveling with small children, please come to the gate at this time."

"I could stay here and track her."

"Go to Phoenix. I'll work this out."

Samantha crossed her arms over her chest. He made this impossible. Her mind spun in a thousand directions. Why was Lisa always trying to get her to stay in New Orleans?

"They're boarding now."

Samantha snapped back to reality. Kevin looked really good with his clean shave and dark blue eyes. The intensity of his stare made her toes tingle.

"Here," he said, slipping her some cash. "You might want a drink or something.

She took the money and shoved it into her pocket. "I think you're wrong."

Kevin leaned in and gently bit her ear. "This will be cleaned up soon."

Samantha took a long, deep breath and stood up. The sunlight cast patches of shadow on the blue berber carpet. She didn't look back as she passed by the boarding attendant. Life was about moving ahead and staying alive—particularly her life.

Chapter Nine

Samantha walked through the security area at the Phoenix airport, and her mood swung from below zero to hovering above bearable. He stood like a rock if a rock wore an orange rugby shirt and jeans. His brown hair appeared to have been combed with his fingers, and a two-day stubble on his face suggested, that at one point while she was gone, he had attempted to do some grooming. He reminded her of one of those Greek statues with the chiseled features. She could see him holding a sword ready to slice someone's head off, while wearing a toga. Jack jutted his chin out at her as they fell in step together.

"How was New Orleans?"

"Ugh, James got killed." There was no way to avoid the sour feeling she got in the pit of her stomach. Something really wrong existed in New Orleans and damned if she could figure it out.

"Yeah, I heard. I guess Kevin took it pretty hard, huh?" Samantha shrugged. "Hard to tell."

"So I guess you had to ditch your gun and knife?"

Samantha cringed. "We left James in a parked car outside a restaurant and caught the first flight out."

"No, you took the first flight out. Where did Kevin go?" Jack pushed the up button on the elevator.

A college kid loaded down with a backpack stepped off the elevator followed by his parents. It must be time for him to head back off to school. It must be nice.

They stepped inside the elevator, and Jack pushed the fifth floor button. He raised his eyebrows at her when she didn't answer.

"Does it matter where he went? He thinks he's better off going solo with no one knowing his destination."

"So he sent you back while he went to New York." Jack scratched his chin and stepped out of the elevator.

"I never said that," Samantha huffed from behind him, having to pick up her pace to keep up with his stride.

Jack got into his pickup without a backwards glance. Samantha stomped around to the passenger side. His newest pickup was dent free, so far, with a shiny grey paint job, and when she opened the door, she marveled that it didn't even smell like tacos. "So why do you think he would go to New York?"

Jack pulled out a cigarette, stuck it in his mouth, and lit it, inhaling deeply. "Just a guess."

Samantha stared at him, wondering how he had managed not to have his nose broken in a million pieces. Probably, because he beat the crap out of most people that tried. Most certainly a lot of people had tried.

Jack grimaced and then pursed his lips. "He has a girlfriend named Evie. She lives in New York."

Samantha snorted. A fleeting sensation of fire and ice ripped through her. That was fine. She focused on the spiraling cement walls as they drove out of the airport-parking garage. She needed to get her head screwed back on. What happened with James had left her completely violated. Lisa had to be behind this. Maybe she should go back to New Orleans and get rid of her. But why should she do that? So Kevin could take it easy in New York with Evie. Samantha rolled down her window. A cool crisp breeze caught her hair, blowing it around.

Jack paid the toll to the airport-parking attendant and caught the freeway heading west.

"Where are we going, anyway?"

"Believe it or not, you're not the only one with problems," he said, switching lanes and checking his rearview mirror.

"What did I miss?"

Jack shrugged. "Getting mixed up with Becki doesn't seem to be working out so well."

Samantha gaped at him. Since the whole thing with Lisa, she really hadn't given that much thought to Becki. Of course, Lisa did work for Becki's family. Maybe they were in on it together. "Why?"

"She wants more and more stuff done."

"Like?"

"Like, if I take a walk for a while, you'll know I'm busy."

Samantha closed her mouth unable to fathom what would happen to Jack. "Won't Mr. Thompson have you killed for working both sides?"

"Not if I do it right." Jack smashed his cigarette out in the ashtray.

Samantha stuck her nose out the window to avoid the stink. The freeway wove its way through the hills as they took a route she had never been on before. They drove north on the 51, and the view revealed rolling hills with small shrub bushes and larger purple mountains in the background.

They finally pulled into a strip mall, and Samantha rolled her eyes not knowing if they had stopped for mexican food or sex toys at Fascinations.

Jack reached under the seat and produced a holster, a gun and a knife—exactly like the ones she had dumped in the New Orleans airport. The .45 was an automatic sub compact, which in retrospect, she probably wouldn't have picked it out herself, but since Jack always supplied the guns and ammo, she had grown used to using it. She took off her jacket, secured the holster and slipped the .45 into place. Now things felt like they were starting to level out. It felt good to be away from all that crap in New Orleans, including Kevin. No, not including Kevin. Hell if she knew. The 3 inch double bladed knife fit into her boot perfectly—ready as she would ever be.

Jack had already gotten out of the truck. It looked like Fascinations had won out over mexican food, but then he kept walking. Samantha got out and followed him. He walked all the way to the end of the strip mall and entered a bookstore.

The sign on the door read Dog-Eared Pages Used Books. Well, this was a new one. She stepped in, leaving the door open.

The woman behind the counter was leaning over it with her eyes narrowed. Her hands were curled into fists on her hips, and she never bothered to take her lethal gaze off of Jack. "You know what you remind me of, Jack," she said between clenched teeth, "a venereal disease that doesn't know when to take penicillin."

Jack smiled his famous shit-eating grin. "April, Samantha, Samantha, April."

April pursed her glossy lips and swung her gaze to Samantha; then she ducked behind the counter and came up with a .44 magnum. The bullet breezed straight out the door right between Jack and Samantha. April's hands flew up in the air, barely holding on to the gun.

The blast roared in Samantha's ears, leaving her ears ringing, and she could almost taste the gunpowder as the bullet streaked past. A scream erupted from outside the store. As Samantha whipped her gun out, she noticed April had put the magnum down on the counter and was yelling at the top of her lungs, while wiping her red curly bangs out of her eyes. "Yeah, you better go home, and don't come back again."

Samantha swiveled to see a guy limping away towards a blue and white station wagon. He dove into the passenger side door, and the driver sped out of the parking lot, leaving a trail of burning rubber.

Samantha put her gun back into her holster. Shaking her head back and forth, she looked from Jack to the absolutely insane woman behind the counter.

With slow and careful movements, Jack reached into his back pocket, taking out a plain white envelope. "I'm glad you finally took those shooting lessons Bruno wanted you to take."

April grinned so wide it even made her eyes light up. "I never took lessons. I'd just as soon shoot you as anyone." April crossed her arms over her chest. "Now what brings you by, Jack? Did you come to pick out a book?"

Jack swallowed. "Always a pleasure, April." He cautiously laid the envelope on the counter beside the .44. "Bruno says he misses you, and I have to ask, why do you keep a gun under the counter?"

April shook her head. "That weirdo has been following me around for a week now. I figured it was high time to give him notice."

"I'll tell, Bruno," Jack said as he turned and started for the door.

"If you tell Bruno, I swear I'll plant a bullet right between your shoulder blades. You better not, Jack. I absolutely will not ..."

But Jack had already ducked out the door and was headed across the parking lot.

April slapped the counter and blew a loose curl up out of her face. She rolled her shoulders. "What's a girl to do?"

Samantha's smile waned, and she bolted out the door to catch up to Jack, hoping she didn't get tagged on the way out. She climbed in, slammed the door and tried to keep her eyeballs from bugging out of her head.

Jack gave her a sideways grin around his cigarette. "Bruno wants to get back together with her so bad he can taste it. I drop off his alimony for him because April can be a little unpredictable. I guess lucky for us she had someone else to let her frustration out on.

"I never knew the bookstore business could be so brutal."

"You have no idea," Jack said, shaking his head sadly. "I used to date a librarian." Jack drew his eyebrows together and then broke out laughing so hard the pickup shook.

Samantha joined him. It was good to be back.

Chapter Ten

The sound of her knuckles cracking reverberated in the empty house. There was no place to conceal her gun. Surprisingly enough it didn't fit in her bra. The red dress she had picked up the last time she was in Mexico clung to every curve imaginable. If only she could've gone shopping and maybe bought a shawl or something, but no.... Jack had dropped her off at home, insisting she had to get ready for Mr. Thompson and Cynthia's engagement party. Samantha could only imagine what kind of party it would be on New Year's Day. Would anyone come, or was that why they threw a last minute party to keep the head count low? Regardless, it looked like everyone expected her to be there.

Grasping her gun in one hand, she glared at her cell phone, before scooping it up along with her keys. Kevin hadn't called, and she refused to call him. What if he really did go to New York to see Evie? How stupid was she?

She backed the Cadillac out of the garage and let the door roll all the way down until it completely closed. Her foot tapped the pedal impatiently as she waited for one of her neighbors to move his slow butt out of her way. Her stomach was in knots. At first, she had been glad to get away from Kevin and let her head clear, but by the time she had finished dressing for the party, she wished he would call. Maybe she could have a beer at the party. Or maybe Bruno could share his love story about him and April, and that would make Samantha feel a hell of a lot better about her love life.

Winding her way through the hills to the mansion didn't take much more time than it did for two songs to play on the radio. She really didn't like parties, and without Kevin, she didn't feel like this one would be any fun. After turning off Happy Valley Road, the hills began to slowly close in around her, becoming a canyon with cacti and some kind of scrub brush dotting the landscape. As she popped over the last dip in the road, she had to stomp on the brakes to keep from hitting the row of cars in front of her. Perhaps, some people were partied out from the night before, but this had the potential to be a rager.

Ken stood by the opening of the wrought iron gate, waving everyone in. The black tuxedo he wore fit him snuggly enough to reveal the bulge of his gun. He lifted his chin in acknowledgement and stuck a finger in his dress shirt collar as if to get some relief.

Luminaries lined the brick road; not to mention the three stories of luminaries that lit up the roof line and every balcony of the mansion, blazing their brilliance into the darkness with no lights on inside to dim them. The effect of no backlights was beautiful, but how could you have a party in the dark? She drove into the underground parking garage and noticed the usually vastly empty garage now offered very few available spaces.

Parking her Cadillac, she sighed, thankful that she could pull into the party with a classy car; instead of hoping, no one saw her when she got out. She clutched her gun, not knowing whether to bring it inside or leave it in the car. Who was she kidding? She didn't even have an evening bag for her keys. O.K., enough drama. She wasn't going to carry the gun around with her. Hiding her keys and gun under the front seat of the car, she crossed her fingers that no one would try to steal her car.

Allen stood by a side door at the end of the garage. He looked a little bit more animated than Ken had as he greeted the guests and directed them onto the walkway that ran along the outside of the mansion. "You look delicious," he said, licking his lips.

Samantha repressed a shiver and tried to ignore his not-so-subtle innuendo.

Allen shrugged, looking every bit the well-dressed villain with his short blonde hair perfectly combed to the side and his black tux exemplifying his small features. "Enjoy it while you can."

The side of the house sported large round paper lights in multi-colors that hung in the air, making rings of light on the grass and the drooping bottleneck trees. The night swayed with an illusion of reality crossing over into a dream; it made the hair on the back of her neck stand up. Not a good sign.

She followed the trail of glitzy guests with all the women under 25, or at least, having received enough plastic surgery that they appeared to be under 25. At the end of the bricked path, the backyard opened up, revealing a huge white tent with light shining out of the entrance. Stopping on the grassy hill, she stepped off to the side and watched as the hundred or so guests milling around slowly made their way into the tent. Soft strains of jazz floated in the air, lending to the false tranquility of the night. For a brief moment, joy rippled through her when a pair of strong arms wrapped around her waist from behind and pulled her to him.

"Miss me?" Kevin whispered into her ear.

She twisted in his arms, skipping over the relief that bloomed inside her, and clung to an emotion she felt more comfortable with—she picked anger. "Why did you go to New York?" Her eyes narrowed as she began scrutinizing his appearance.

Kevin smoothed a strand of hair out of her face. "That's where the laundry houses are and where Sal is. I thought maybe I'd be able to piece together something about the laundry houses before anyone caught me."

"And what about Evie?"

Kevin took a step back as if he had been hit. His features looked raw and pain flitted across his face. "I went to see Evie," his voice cracked, and his eyes shifted away from Samantha's. "I wanted to ask her a few questions, but I never got to. She was dead when I got there."

Samantha felt a torrent of emotion slide through her—anger, betrayal, sorrow (for her or Kevin she didn't know). "If Evie was alive, would you be here?"

"It depends on what she told me." He took one of her hands in his, barely holding it with his fingertips.

Even in the dim light, his eyes looked red. Samantha wanted to jerk away from him. One side of her agreed with his logic, and the other side screamed betrayal.

Kevin brought his face down until he was a mere inch away from her face. "Because I went to her apartment, I'm now wanted for questioning in the murder investigation of Evie Bryson. If I didn't have good connections with the New York City Police, I would be in a jail cell right now. Someone is setting me up hard—someone who knows my patterns."

"So what did you want to ..." Samantha jumped when an elegantly dressed man appeared beside Kevin and clapped a hand on his back. It took a minute for Samantha to place him, she had been so wrapped up in Kevin that the party hadn't existed.

"Good evening, Kevin, Samantha." Carlos Antigos (Mr. Thompson and Kevin's friend, partner, whatever) flashed a smile full of white teeth that sparkled almost as brightly as his diamond earring. "If the two of you have a lot more fighting to do, I would postpone it until after all the toasts have been made for Brody and Cynthia." He let his hand drop from Kevin's back and walked down the sloping grass towards the tent.

Samantha felt like the roots of her hair were on fire. Wow, that arrogant piece of crap pissed her off. The last time she had seen Carlos he had sent her to the warehouse where she got her head beat in. Turning her anger on Kevin, she poked him in the chest with her finger. "So what were you going to ask Evie? And one more thing, it's obvious you and Becki didn't have an exclusive relationship. I know for a fact she was seeing Ani Goro and you at the same time."

His eyes blazed with a cold intensity. "This isn't over, and until it is, you're not leaving my side." He tucked her arm around his and began to guide her in the direction of the tent.

Samantha tried to jerk away from him, but he tightened his hold on her by locking his hand around her fingers and squeezing. Forcing back the urge to punch him, she walked in with him, trying to keep as much distance from him as possible while her right arm remained intertwined with his.

Inside the chandelier lights twinkled, and candles on every table flickered, bathing the whole tent with a warm glow. Mr. Thompson and Cynthia sat at a large table in the middle of the room. Cynthia had gone all out with her red hair twisted into an elaborate updo complete with sparkles to match her dress. Samantha attempted a tight lip smile as she and Kevin made their way to the empty seats next to Cynthia. Well, at least, no one would accuse her of trying to upstage the bride-to-be.

Jack sat at a table behind Mr. Thompson, looking dapper and disgruntled at the same time. His short hair looked as if he might have sprung for a haircut and shave. The black tux had grey lapels, and his white shirt buttoned to the throat with little black buttons lining the front of it. His eyes followed her and Kevin, and Samantha felt them burning into her back when she sat down.

Four other men sat at the table with him—all of them gunmen. Samantha suspected Carlos had brought a couple of guys with him. The two guys to the left of Jack even looked slightly familiar. Maybe they had been at Carlos's house last time she was in Mexico City. She didn't like having so many gunmen sitting behind her even if one of them was Jack, and who needed enough protection to bring another two gunmen? She scanned the room quickly but couldn't find Bruno. Why should that make her uneasy? Usually, it was the opposite, being around him made her feel nervous.

Kevin pulled the seat next to Cynthia out for her, which placed her directly across from Carlos. Samantha threw one last hate-filled glance at Kevin, before taking her seat. Carlos smirked at her and continued his conversation with Mr. Thompson as Carlos's date smiled her plastic red lipstick smile, which was only barely upstaged by her plunging neckline.

Samantha jumped when Kevin's hand touched the back of her neck and started making small circles with his thumb. She sucked in a breath to keep from screaming. Turning sideways in her chair, she gave him her best cut-the-crap look but to no avail. Kevin winked at her and continued lightly touching her. Carlos snickered, and she couldn't help but throw daggers with her eyes at him. He beamed and then placed his hand on the back of his date's neck and began doing the same thing.

Cynthia nudged her in the side. "I think for a last minute bash this is a really good turnout."

The distraction couldn't have come at a better time. Samantha felt her feelings getting cross-threaded some-where between screaming mad and ripping clothes off sex. "Wow, I guess. You look amazing."

"Well, I forced the fabulous; I spent all day yesterday, getting every part of me resurfaced. I spent 10 hours at the spa. When I got home last night, I was nothing but jelly." Cynthia leaned in closer and lowered her voice, "I heard you guys had some trouble in New Orleans."

Samantha drew in a slow cleansing breath and forced herself to quit playing with her napkin. Kevin's hand started drifting from her neck down her bare back, following the strap all the way to her waist. Repressing a shiver, she leaned back in her chair in an attempt to smash his hand. "We did have a couple of shooting incidents. I guess you heard about James."

Cynthia shook her head, her green eyes wide with compassion. "I'm certain that if you had been with James he would definitely still be alive."

Samantha knew the instant Mr. Thompson turned his steely grey eyes in her direction. Her heart skipped a beat. Was he angry with her about James? She nodded her agreement with Cynthia and looked down at the plate, which had been set in front of her. Stuffed lobster, scallops, twice baked potatoes, and peas with artichoke hearts stared back at her. Cynthia hadn't seen her break down in New Orleans, but Samantha felt the guilt twist in her stomach. Maybe she hadn't been around to save James, but what if they had shot Kevin while she had been swimming in her panic attack. She looked up at Kevin, who had been watching her the whole time. He needed her. She knew that. The only question was would she be tough enough to keep him alive. Samantha picked at her food and sipped her champagne.

The after dinner toasts lasted long enough for the alcohol to go to her head. The party whirled around her as she sat completely numb to the whole affair. She felt Kevin take her hand and looked up to see his dark blue eyes so close to her that the intensity traveled all the way to her toes.

"Let's go dance," he whispered.

She followed Kevin out the back of the tent, feeling Jack's eyes on her. A large wooden dance floor had been resurrected 100 feet from the tent with tiny paper lights illuminating the entire area.

When they reached the dance floor, Samantha stood perfectly still, trying to juggle the barrage of emotions that continued to divide her. Kevin reached out; his fingers wrapped around her waist and drew her to him slowly until their bodies met. They barely swayed to the moonlight melodies. "You're right. Becki and I weren't exclusive. I never really knew who she was seeing, but I always suspected."

"And you were with Evie?"

"Some." Kevin looked far away and then back to Samantha. "Evie and I were also friends. I went to see her, wondering if she had somehow had a hand with the laundry houses or maybe knew something that I didn't. She kept herself fairly well connected with a lot of powerful men in New York, but what I found makes me sick."

"Do you know for sure it had something to do with you, or could Evie's lifestyle have brought this on?"

Kevin brought his head down so it was even with Samantha's. "Either I'm the unluckiest bastard there is, or she was killed to set me up. Right after I left her apartment, I got a call from my buddy telling me the cops had put an APB out for me. That's when I said forget it and got a friend of mine to fly me back here in a private plane. So here I am with my girlfriend pissed off and the cops aching to catch up to me."

Samantha put her head on his shoulder, soaking up his scent—a combination of clean and strong and home. She knew without being told that Kevin hadn't killed Evie— no more so than he had killed James. His life was spiraling out of control at a record rate.

"There's Carlos. I need to find out something real quick," Kevin said, leading Samantha off the dance floor.

Away from the space heaters, Samantha felt goose bumps up and down her arms. The night wasn't particularly cold for January, but still most people had jackets or mink wraps, except for her of course. As they approached the tent, Samantha spotted Jack having a smoke on the west side of the lawn. Giving Kevin's hand a quick squeeze, she set off across the grass.

"Why aren't you shadowing Mr. Thompson?"

Jack dropped his cigarette in the grass and snuffed it out with his foot. "Because one of Sal's gunmen left the tent, and I'm standing out here to make sure he doesn't come back with an uzi."

"Sounds practical, but if he comes back with an uzi what are you going to do?"

"Shoot him, or at least, scream before I die."

"Wow, great job you have, Jack. Don't suppose you know where I could apply?"

"So how come Kevin's here and not New York?"

Samantha watched the leaves of a tree sway as a breeze kicked up. "I guess the New York cops are after him. He found Evie dead. How about Becki? Any news from her?"

"Nope, I want you to do me a favor…. Let Kevin go."

It felt like a slap out of nowhere. "Let Kevin go where?" Samantha's voice shook as she tried to reign in her anger.

Jack tilted her chin up even more, and she found herself staring into his liquid brown eyes. "When a locomotive is headed right for you, you should get off the tracks."

Samantha's heart hammered in her chest. She thought for sure he was going to kiss her. He was so close; she could smell his cologne—a mixture of rain and earth and grass all rolled into one. Then just like that his hand fell away, and he stalked off.

Samantha stood in the grass, listening to a cricket that had struck up its own song, while the band took a break. Why was everything Jack said so cryptic? Logic and reason made sense to her—but not Jack.

Kevin, Carlos and Antoinette, Carlos's date, came out of the tent trailed by two gunmen. They walked up the lawn until they met the path that led to the garage. Kevin broke away from the group and strode over to Samantha. "I have to go with Carlos for a while."

Samantha sputtered. Her throat felt tight and suddenly she shivered. "Do you really think that's best?" The darkness hid her misty eyes. The whine in her voice was unmistakable, but at least it was a step above crying.

"Most definitely. The body count keeps rising, but I'll be a lot harder to get to from now on. I think you should stay here at the mansion. I don't want you to be alone at your house."

The band started up again, and Samantha looked over Kevin's shoulder, not daring to look into his eyes. "Be safe," she whispered to Kevin as she turned to go up the hill towards the mansion. She wanted to escape. An overwhelming feeling of loss spread through her, making her heart pound in her ears and a feeling of nausea seize her.

He gently pulled her to him. "Don't make me regret this," he growled. Neither of them moved, frozen for a moment, wanting nothing more than the present to last longer. Then he kissed her forehead and took off to follow Carlos and his crew.

As she watched him go, everything became crystal clear. Maybe Kevin didn't need someone to protect him; maybe he needed someone to do his hunting.

Chapter Eleven

It felt like a fire had been lit under her. Ever since Ani had been shot, she had been drifting, wondering what the next step was. Torn between staying with these sociopaths and wading through the muck to save Kevin, she now knew exactly what to do. He didn't need someone watching his back; he needed someone to do some cleaning.

She stuck her head inside the tent, but couldn't find Jack anywhere. Brody and Cynthia were at the table, chatting it up with a group of people Samantha had never seen before. There was no Jack or Bruno; in fact all of the bodyguards were gone. Ducking out before anyone saw her, she moved in the direction of the dance floor. Traipsing around in heels made her paranoid, the thought of her getting her shoe stuck and landing face down seemed completely probable.

Lots of couples swayed to the smooth tempo, but she didn't see Jack. He hadn't gone into the mansion either. The firing range would be a strange place for all of them to disappear to, but maybe there was trouble. She skirted around the dance floor, walking as quickly as she could with a long dress and high heels down a dirt path. At the back of the property, a large wooden fence covered in a vine hid the shooting range. As she got closer, she could hear them taunting each other.

"Move the target farther back. I'm not your cross-eyed mama."

Samantha opened the gate and found Jack, Bruno and two of the men that had sat with Jack at dinner.

"And here's my girl. Come over here, Samantha, and show these monkeys how to shoot."

Grinding her teeth, she took the gun Jack had extended to her. He moved aside, letting her step closer to the table. A single playing card 50 yards away had been clipped into the carrier, which normally held a full size target. The floodlights barely illuminated the card. Samantha wondered if she should hit the top spade on the two of spades or the bottom spade. Since she didn't really care, she fired twice.

One of the guys laughed. Samantha glanced at him, and their eyes locked for a second. Some might mistake him for handsome: about her height, dark hair cut short, and the kind of features that said no bullshit. "Don't worry if you missed it. It's dark out, anyway. Name's Dana."

"Samantha," she said, placing the gun on the table and shaking his hand.

Jack whistled as he pulled the card from the metal clip. "Yeah, it's not so dark she didn't hit it bull's eye twice."

He handed the card to Dana, who studied the perfect hole in the middle of each spade.

"Crap, with your big mouth, Jack, how long do you think she'll keep you alive?"

"I'm a handy sort of guy," Jack said, grinning. "It's your turn to shoot." He stepped out of the way and sauntered over to the fence, leaning his back against it.

Samantha followed him. "You never said where Becki took off to."

Jack shook his head. "What I said was, 'if you're standing in front of a train get off the tracks.'"

"That's not going to work for me."

Jack snorted, "Now how did I know that."

Samantha knew without being told two times in one night that Jack wasn't going to give her any more information. Jack had helped her track down Ani by befriending Becki. Supposedly, he got paid to do nothing. Which equated to when Mr. Thompson gave him a job, Becki might tell Jack to do nothing, or maybe there would come a time when Becki would have a job of her own for him.

Guilt slithered through her stomach. Glancing up, she took in Jack's roman nose with its slight hump. He was smiling at the other gunman, who was apparently trying to attach the playing card horizontally to see if anyone could separate the card with a bullet. She had put Jack in this position, but if Becki wasn't around anymore, Jack's position wouldn't be compromised.

"You do it, Samantha," Jack said, giving her a small jab in the arm.

She looked up to find four sets of eyes watching her. Bruno held the gun out for her. He gave her a slight head bow as she took the gun from him.

Out of the corner of her eye, she could see the gunman, who had attached the playing card, staring at her intensely. He was a small guy with a foxy demeanor. Samantha watched him as he moved about five feet away, putting himself in the shadows of the floodlights. Something about him made her skin crawl. As soon as she shot this stupid card, she was leaving. She refused to get suckered into a quick draw contest with these guys.

The card hung at least as far out as the two of spades had been if not a little farther. She picked up the gun, placing her left hand underneath her right. Her arms shook a little bit due to the cold night air. The warming effects of Kevin and the champagne had disappeared.

A movement so fast she didn't have time to blink caused her internal warning system to start screaming. The gunman, who had positioned himself on her right side in the shadows, drew his gun. Samantha started to turn her gun on him when she felt a strong hand push her down onto the table, and a loud pop rang in her ears as a bullet whizzed over her, catching the gunman square in the left side of his chest. Two more shots ripped through the night. One of the shots she knew came from Bruno because he kept his hand on her, pinning her to the table. She watched Bruno's second bullet hit the gunman in the head before he fell to the ground.

Panic streaked through her, making her twist out from under Bruno's grasp until she could see Jack.

Jack lowered his gun slowly, never taking his eyes off of Dana, who now lay on the ground with his legs bent at an odd angle and a gun still clamped in his fingers.

Her heart pounded out of control. The sound of the band in the distance floated in the silence as if the notes hung suspended in the air. Had anyone at the party heard the gunshots? Unconsciously, she placed the gun in her hand on the table and continued to stare at the dead guy on the ground.

Jack re-holstered his gun and brushed his hand down his white shirt in a thoughtless gesture. "You thought I got shot."

"Don't be ridiculous," Samantha snapped.

"Then why did you twist away from Bruno to look at me?" Jack smirked. "You got dust all over the front of your dress."

"Sorry about that. You are so very pulchritudinous," Bruno said, brushing his hand over the thin fabric that covered her breasts. After a couple of pats, he gave up and began to pick at the top of her dress, trying to eradicate the dust particles one at a time.

"Thanks," Samantha mumbled, grabbing his hands in midair before he could continue with the groping. She let go of his hands and took a step backwards.

Bruno shrugged, turned red and walked over to pick up the gun from the dead guys hand. Jack couldn't quit laughing. He shook all over, not even trying to hide his amusement.

"Why don't you and Samantha tell Mr. Thompson what happened while I go out the back way and take care of the bodies."

Jack shuddered, trying to get his giggles under control. "You need help loading?"

"No, but get a clean gun."

Jack pulled his gun out, put it down on the table, and picked another one up out of a silver case, which had been lying out. He shoved the gun in his holster. "Let's go," he said as he started for the gate.

Bruno disappeared out of sight, which was weird considering there wasn't really anything back here except open desert. The two bodies lay sprawled on the ground. Kevin had been right; if she was going to stay alive, she needed Jack and Bruno.

Samantha stumbled, trying to keep up with Jack's long stride.

Stopping in the middle of the path, Jack waited for Samantha to catch up. He caught her arm in his and began walking towards the tent at a slower pace. The music had continued to play as if no one had heard the gunshots, either that, or no one wanted to know what happened.

"Why did those guys start shooting?" Samantha demanded.

"That's what we're going to find out. Both of those guys worked for Sal. By the way, I really like that dress."

Samantha ignored him. He was still grinning because Bruno had copped a feel.

Inside the tent, Mr. Thompson and Cynthia were still sitting at the table, but now they were entertaining a thin man with hair slicked back in a ponytail and a date that looked about 18 (maybe).

Jack strode over to their table and leaned in, speaking to Mr. Thompson. He kept his voice low, but the effect it had on the whole table was obvious. Mr. Thompson stood up, taking Cynthia's arm and helping her out of her chair. The guy with the ponytail picked up the shot glass in front of him, emptied it, and thumped it back down on the table. With Mr. Thompson and Cynthia taking the lead, Jack and Samantha flanked the other two as they left the tent and ambled to the mansion.

Once the door closed and they were all inside, the silence became thick enough to hear a drop of sweat roll off of someone. Jack pressed the hidden elevator button in the hall. "Go ahead," Jack said, looking at Samantha. "Sal and I will wait."

Mr. Thompson and Cynthia stepped into the elevator followed by Samantha. Sal's date started to follow, but Jack put a hand on her shoulder. "You can wait here with us."

The girl inched closer to Sal, her bottom lip trembling and her dark eyes blinking rapidly.

Samantha kept her gaze on the pair until the doors closed. This had to be Sal from New York—the one who knew about the laundry houses that Kevin had been blamed for setting up.

"What happened?" Mr. Thompson demanded as the elevator zipped up one floor.

"One or both of Sal's guys opened fire on us. Bruno took care of one, and Jack took out the other."

The elevator door opened into the reception area. Not one paper or sticky note lay out on Bruno's desk. In fact, the only thing on the desk was a phone, and behind the desk a row of filing cabinets that lined the back wall with only a lone fax machine sitting out.

"Cynthia, take the other elevator upstairs."

Cynthia stepped away from Mr. Thompson with her eyes slit like a cobras. "I'm a part of this, too, you know. I don't think sending me away every time something comes up is the answer."

Mr. Thompson gently stroked Cynthia's cheek. "Go upstairs," he said, and then he dropped his hand from her cheek, striding into the conference room without a backwards glance.

Cynthia's mouth snapped shut in a hard line. Her green eyes darkened, and her dangling diamond earrings shook. With a swish of blue silk, she stalked off around the corner.

Samantha let out a breath. No matter what, she didn't want to get caught in the middle of a fight between Mr. Thompson and Cynthia. It would be a no-win situation, that was for sure.

The elevator doors opened, and Jack along with his two new buddies in tow exited the elevator. Samantha waited for the three of them to pass and then followed everyone into the conference room, closing the door behind her. Mr. Thompson sat at the head of the table with his elbows propped on it and his fingers laced together.

Sal went straight to the liquor cabinet and poured himself what looked like a double shot. "What the hell is this, Jack? You break up a nice party for what? Can't you see your boss is getting married?" He pulled a chair out and took a seat between Mr. Thompson and his date.

The dark haired girl took to tapping her nails on the table until Sal reached over and put a hand on top of hers.

"Dana and Vince got taken out a few minutes ago," Jack said as he glared at him from across the table. Towering above everyone, Jack looked ready to pounce on top of Sal either with fists or bullets but definitely by force.

"What the hell kind of set up are you running here? I knew things weren't right with all this crap Kevin is involved in, but you can't invite me to a party and have me taken out. This is crap." Sal knocked his chair backwards onto the floor as he stood up, stumbled around the chair and began to pace.

Jack held up his large hands. "Don't play like you didn't know. They drew their guns on me first. I think Samantha was the target."

Mr. Thompson and Sal turned their attention to Samantha. She had kept post at the door and now felt the blood drain from her face. How had she missed the fact that people were actually trying to kill her?

"Why?" Mr. Thompson asked as he rubbed his goatee.

Jack shrugged. "Because she shot Ani."

Mr. Thompson looked at Sal, who was shaking his head and stuffing his hands in his pockets. "I never told them to shoot anyone," Sal said, pulling his hands out of his pockets and waving them through the air as if to dismiss the whole thing. "We were here to have a good time and leave. That's it." He stopped pacing and picked the chair up off the floor, shoving it back into place.

His date looked very pale and fragile. She scraped at the pink nail polish on one of her manicured hands and bit the side of her lip. "It was Becki Guerrero." Her voice wavered as she looked up at Samantha and then at Mr. Thompson. "I saw her yesterday at Sal's talking to Dana and Vince. I didn't really hear everything she said, but Dana said, 'No, Sal will kill us.' Then Becki told him, 'Don't worry. It will be well worth your effort.'"

Sal reached out with his right hand and backslapped the girl so hard her neck snapped back and then forward. Sal jerked the chair backwards and hauled the girl up by her arm. "You better be right because you're sentencing Becki Guerrero to death." He began pulling the girl along with him as he marched towards the door. "You can shoot me in the back, Jack, or I'm leaving—either way."

Samantha stood in front of the door, frozen, her eyes glued to Sal and the girl. Behind them, Mr. Thompson motioned with his hand for her to step aside.

"Jack walk Sal and his date to their car."

The girl never looked at Samantha. Tears ran down her face, making track marks in her makeup. Her mouth looked red and puffy. Sal's jaw clenched and unclenched, and his skin had turned an ashen color. A wave of fear floated around them as Sal hurriedly threw open the door in a panic to get away.

"Sal," Mr. Thompson's voice stopped him before he could make his escape to the reception area.

Sal turned around slowly, never loosening his grip on the girl's arm.

"What happened here tonight never leaves this room, or you and your girl sentenced yourselves to death. The way I see it is your boys took a vacation."

Sal nodded and jerked the girl along with him. Jack passed by Samantha, keeping his full attention on Sal.

The elevator doors took their time closing, and Mr. Thompson continued to stare long after all three of them had departed. Finally, he turned his gaze to Samantha. "I can't take out Becki Guerrero without starting a war with José Guerrero, and wars don't make money, only blood."

Samantha nodded her head up and down. She couldn't believe Sal had hit that little girl, but hadn't she come up here half-expecting Sal to get shot? Was Jack really walking them to their car?

"I think you and Jack need to take a vacation."

All the rambling in her head screeched to a halt. Did Mr. Thompson tell her exactly what she wanted to hear? Excitement raced through her, and she didn't dare breathe.

He got up from the table, walked over to the liquor cabinet, and poured a shot. Then he turned one of the Chinese Sumo wrestler statues that stood on the cabinet. A large section of the wall swung open, revealing a safe.

"I know it's not very original, but I don't keep that much money in here, anyway." He pulled a big wad of bills out and crossed back to Samantha.

She hadn't moved from her spot by the door. Everything was coming together. With a shaky hand, she reached out and wrapped her fingers around the money. Blood money—money to take care of Becki, to protect to Kevin, to help Jack. Amazing how simple rationalizing the unthinkable had become.

Mr. Thompson's grey eyes cut into her. "If you and Jack get into trouble, there's no one you can call."

Samantha shook her head up and down.

"Here, I think there are some trash bags you can wrap your money in." He strode into the outer office and opened a drawer, pulling out a roll of blue trash bags. Tearing one off, he handed it to Samantha. "Find Jack and get out of here. Don't talk to anyone. Just leave."

Samantha shoved the cash in the bag and wrapped the plastic around itself. She shrugged, unsure what needed to be said if anything. "Tell Kevin I'll be in touch."

Mr. Thompson smiled, erasing the hardness he often projected. "I will."

Chapter Twelve

The elevator doors shut, and Samantha banged her head back against the mirrored wall. How could she be so dumb? Her boss wasn't a delivery boy. Couldn't she have thought of anything else to say?

When she stepped out of the elevator into the hall, she heard Jack arguing with someone.

"I told you not to call me until later tonight. Yeah, I know what you want. I'll get back to you later."

Samantha came into the kitchen, wishing (not the first time tonight) that she had her gun. "Hey Jack, let's get going."

Jack spun around, clicking his phone off. "Where," he snapped?

"To my house," Samantha said, keeping her voice down in case someone overheard them.

Jack didn't move. He stared at her, his eyebrows arching up, practically touching.

She blew out an exasperated breath and then winked several times.

Jack grunted, grabbed her hand and led her into the den right off the hall. The dark room made Samantha nervous. Without being overly obvious, she kept as close to Jack as possible. He opened his bedroom door, pulled her in and shut the door behind him. "What?"

"Can you turn on the light, please?"

Jack hit the switch, and the brightness caused Samantha to blink. "I told you, let's go to my house."

"There's no camera or listening device in here. I ripped those out right after they put them in."

Samantha tapped her foot on the thick shag carpeting. "You and I are supposed to take a vacation." She held up the money in the plastic bag. "It's cash, and if we need help, there's no one to call."

Jack took the wad of cash, weighed it in his hand and then gave it back. "Nice. Well, just so you know your house is monitored, too. So the next time we have to have a top-secret meeting it should be outside or in my room. Which by the way, since we're on vacation, you want to pull that dress off and hop into bed."

"Man, I wish had worn my gun."

"I'll change. I'm not wearing this monkey suit all night." Jack grabbed a few things from his closet and went into the bathroom, closing the door behind him.

Samantha sat down on the unmade bed. The room looked a lot like the one she had stayed in when she first came to work for Mr. Thompson. It had a large bed in one corner, and two dark recliners took up the opposite corners of the room. Jack had added his own mini-fridge, which would defeat the purpose of walking the 15 feet out to the den to get a drink or the 30 feet to the kitchen to get something to eat.

She twisted her hands, waiting didn't happen to be one of her strong points. Jack came back in wearing jeans, boots, black t-shirt and a black hunting vest. He rummaged through his closet and finally came out with a duffel bag.

"Are we going to New York?"

Jack shook his head as he reached under the bed, pulling out rolled up socks and sticking them in his bag. "New Orleans."

Samantha felt a chill run through her. "What's in the socks?"

Jack smiled. "For me to know and you to find out."

She didn't think she wanted to find out.

He ducked back into the bathroom, slammed a few more drawers and came out. "O.K., let's roll."

Not a sound could be heard in the dark den. They didn't bother with the lights as they crept out of the den and into the hall. Outside Samantha could see the lights twinkling and the guests roaming around. She hit the number two twice, knowing twenty-two would get her to the garage, and the floor they were on was thirty-one. A smile spread across her face. Twenty-one was the code for the gym, which was on the same level as the garage, but the elevator door opened the opposite way. Forty-six would take them to the offices on the second floor. One of these days, she needed to spend some time exploring that floor. Come to think of it, there was a whole lot of the first floor that she hadn't checked out either. Maybe this gunslinger thing suited her.

No one jumped out from behind one of the cars parked in the overflowing garage to ruin her moment of confidence. "How many cars fit in this place?"

"Fifty—twenty-five on each side."

Jack's boots echoed along with the click of Samantha's heels. A few more feet and she would be inside her car with her gun beside her. She jerked open the door and slid her hand under the seat, feeling the comfort of the cold steel as she wrapped her fingers around it. A sigh escaped her. Part of her brain acknowledged that her behavior wasn't normal, but another side argued that the loss of her immediate family had caused her to seek the comfort of a false sense of security. Samantha raised her eyebrows as she buckled her seat belt. Psychobabble wasn't her favorite topic. Placing the money and gun beside her, she stuck the key in the ignition and fired the car up.

Jack had his phone in his hand and was furiously texting before they even left the garage. His appearance had improved considerably with the hair combing and clean-shaven look. He didn't strike her as being strung out like he had a few days earlier, but his behavior was still off.

"Who are you texting?"

Jack looked Samantha right in the eye with a leer that made her heart skip a couple of beats. "Becki."

"What?"

He pulled out a cigarette from his black hunting vest. "You didn't think she would go away did you? I tried keeping it hushed that you were the one who shot Ani, but that didn't work." His lighter flared in the car, and he rolled down his window as he inhaled. "So there's a leak somewhere, but there always is. Now she wants you dead, and of course, she wants Kevin dead."

"She said that?" Samantha turned on the heater and shivered as it began blowing air on her feet.

"She offered me fifty-thousand apiece for you guys."

Samantha kept her eyes locked on the road ahead with her hands firmly attached to the steering wheel, so Jack couldn't see her shake. She had considered shooting Becki the day she had found her and Ani together outside of Phoenix, but now she sorely wished she had. A quick glance at Jack made her stomach stop flipping. If he had wanted to kill her, he could've let Sal's guys do it—unless he didn't want to share the money. There was no sign of Ken as Samantha stopped to wait for the gate to roll open.

"I figure we'll make it to New Orleans by morning, catch up to Becki and be back by tomorrow evening." He flicked his cigarette ash out the window.

"That easy, huh?"

"Why not?"

The lights of the luminaries glowed behind them as they drove away from the mansion. Samantha shrugged— she knew why because nothing is ever a sure thing. "So why not off Kevin and me? You would be what a hundred thousand ahead of the game? Early retirement?"

"Not enough to get me interested. Mr. Thompson would be pissed if anything ever happened to Kevin."

"Oh, and I'm expendable."

Jack grinned and flipped his cigarette out the window. "Not to me."

She didn't have anything to say to that; instead she rolled down her window in an attempt to air out the car. She tried not to let her anger get the best of her. Wasn't it normal in this business to have a hit put on you? "So how many times has someone tried to kill you off, Jack?"

"I've told you and told you; you have to stay under the radar. But you don't listen. I stay under the radar."

Samantha rolled her eyes. "Like last month when Dominique Francizzi tried to kill you in the hot tub?"

"That wasn't because he had a hit out on me."

"Still, not what I would call, 'staying under the radar.'"

The buzzing of Jack's cell phone in his pocket broke the silence in the car. Samantha ignored the clenching feeling in her gut. This was Jack. And before Jack had been Sam.

Samantha hit the button on the garage door opener and rolled into her parking space beside the pickup. She wanted to deny it, but she really was afraid to come home alone at night; having Jack with her did help a little. She picked up her gun and gripped it tightly as she got out of the car. Cautiously pushing the door from the garage into the dining room open, Samantha paused in the doorway.

A strong stench of cigarette smoke caught her attention, and the smell wasn't coming from Jack. Her eyes flitted from the living room and back to the kitchen, before landing on the bar. A deck of cards had been laid out like a clock on the counter. The barstool, which was normally pushed under the counter, now stuck out from under the bar by about a foot.

Her pulse raced through her as a bead of sweat trailed down her back. She inched closer to the cards, keeping her gun pointed towards the back of the house. Jack had drawn his gun and came to stand beside her as she stared at the cards. She couldn't find any hidden message in the way the cards were arranged. The image of Sam, sitting here on the barstool playing cards, made her head dizzy. If he had been here, why would he leave? Because of Jack—

maybe. She walked into the kitchen and carefully opened the cabinet door under the sink. Shoving her hand into the trash sack, she felt around until she found it. There in the bottom of the trash lay a wet cigarette butt. Samantha spun towards the back of the house and checked the showers, closets, even under her bed.

Jack stood in the doorway of her bedroom, watching her. "Not a big fan of solitaire, huh."

"I think my brother is still alive." The words rushed out of her, leaving her to feel empty and hollow.

Jack shrugged. "What makes you think that?"

"I saw him twice in New Orleans, and now I think he's followed me here."

"You saw him twice?"

Samantha nodded. "The first time was at Kevin's condo on New Year's Eve. He was in the shadows watching us, and then he took off. The second time was right after James got shot. He was across the street."

Jack pulled out a cigarette.

"There's no smoking in here."

"Your brother does."

"Get out of my room." Samantha scooted Jack out and closed the door behind him. Her hand shook as she ran her fingers through her hair. Things would be fine. She didn't know what to think about her brother, but she did know what to think about Becki. Focus—that was all she had to do.

She grabbed her black duffel bag out of the closet and carefully stuffed it full of suits and underwear. She contemplated packing her tennis shoes, but blew it off, knowing there wouldn't be any time to workout. Throwing her bathing suit on top, she added a brush, a travel kit and some makeup (all compliments of Cynthia). Her dress came off in one smooth motion, and Samantha replaced it with a grey silk shirt and matching suit. Tucking her shirt in, she secured her gun in her holster and attached the extra ammo clip. Whoever packed her bag last time hadn't thought to put in extra ammo. Her boots sat in the closet, waiting for her to put them on. She slipped her feet in, checked her knife and stood up. Now she was ready.

"Are we flying or driving?" Samantha asked as she lugged her bag into the kitchen.

"Driving I guess unless…." He scratched his clean-shaven jaw. "Maybe we could fly with Cynthia's sister, Cassi."

"For some reason, that doesn't sound like a good thing. Why didn't I meet her at the party?"

Jack regarded Samantha with one raised eyebrow arched above his piercing brown eyes. "If you bothered to take your eyes off of Kevin, you might have noticed her. Although, I don't see how anyone couldn't have seen her.

She wore a see-through dress complete with pierced nipples and tattoos instead of underwear. Bruno and I studied that pretty hard. The front definitely looks like a heart, and the back must be a dragon."

Samantha jerked her bag up off the floor and marched to the garage, clicking the lights off as she went and letting the door bang shut behind her. She really must be pretty daft to have missed that. It didn't matter what she told herself; the reality was she had it bad for Kevin. And having it bad wasn't always good.

Chapter Thirteen

Jack jumped in the car while Samantha waited for the garage door to open. She wanted to get away from the house and keep on running. A coil of fear wrapped itself around her as she backed out into the street. Was it really her brother or someone trying to play with her mind? Because if it was really him, then it would make more sense that he spoke to her instead of showing up and disappearing all the time. And to have someone in your house when you're not home notched up the creepy factor, ignoring the whole dead brother thing.

"I should make sure it's cool that we catch a ride with her before we show up at the airport and demand to go with her."

"Funny, you know her phone number."

"A heart tattoo and a dragon tattoo. I don't think there's anything more that needs to be said." His voice lowered when someone on the other line answered. "I've been thinking it would be nice to spend some time in New Orleans. What about making room on the plane for me and my partner?"

"No, it's not Bruno. She's the chick that was with Kevin.

Huh, you don't have to tell me." He nodded his head up and down as he listened. "Thanks, we won't hold you up much. We're already en route."

Samantha wanted to ask what she had said but decided to squash her curiosity. What went on between her and Kevin didn't have anything to do with anyone else. She checked her mirror for headlights, but none of the cars behind them seemed very intent on staying close.

"Good thing I called. She's already at the airport. I guess her and Evie were pretty tight along with some of the other girls at the house."

"What house?"

Jack chuckled and shook his head. "Cassi owns a cathouse outside of New Orleans. Evie used to live there before Kevin moved her to New York."

Something foul ripped through her. Her body didn't know whether to heave or pass out. Her hands turned clammy, and she had to wipe her sweaty palms on her pants.

"Everyone in this business has a past, Samantha."

"A past being what—an hour ago?"

Jack opened his mouth and then closed it, shrugging his shoulders as they turned onto the road that led into the airport. "Park over there." Jack pointed to a small parking lot off to the side of an airplane hangar.

Samantha jumped out of the car anxious to feel the cool night breeze on her skin. Breathing deeply, she scanned what she could of the airport. The overhead lights did a good job lighting the immediate area, but past the hangars there appeared to be nothing but darkness. Anyone could be out there, pointing a gun at them right now. She closed her eyes, forcing the paranoia to go away. They had made these plans last minute. Unless someone followed them, it would be unlikely they could be hiding in the desert, waiting to take a shot.

Grabbing the cash, she tucked it into her duffel bag, slung the bag over her shoulder, locked the car up and began walking towards the hangar. Jack strolled beside her, talking on his cell phone. Out of the corner of her eye, Samantha caught sight of a black cat streaking across the pavement right in front of them. Bad enough she had to go back to New Orleans; damn cat.

He clicked his phone off and shoved it into his pocket. "Guissepe is going to have someone drive the car back later." Waving his hand like an idiot, he picked up his pace, so he could grab hold of the jaw-dropping brunette and swing her around in the air.

To Samantha's annoyance, not only was the woman obviously still wearing the see-through dress, she wrapped her arms around Jack, pressing her whole body into his and running her fingers through his short blondish-brown hair. "I'm so glad you're coming home with me," she purred. Turning slightly while still engulfed in Jack's arms, she batted her sea-green eyes at Samantha. "Oh, and you must be Samantha, Kevin's new girlfriend."

The similarity between Cassi and Cynthia couldn't be denied, but Samantha didn't feel any kinship towards Cassi—instead the hair on her neck stood up. "Thanks for letting us hitch a ride with you," Samantha managed to mumble, without showing too much hostility.

"Oh, it's no bother at all," Cassi said, staring up at Jack while she continued to cling to his arm.

Samantha followed behind, watching Cassi's long brown hair sway just above her ass. She couldn't help but try to strain her eyesight to see the tattoo. It could be a dragon if only the lighting attached to the hangers was a little brighter.

Cassi's plane didn't resemble Mr. Thompson's or Kevin's, it looked like porn music would start playing any minute. Samantha craned her head around wondering where the cameras might be. The couches were cream colored with rows of small black skulls running across the fabric. She shook her head, trying to be oblivious to the décor and to the rub down that Jack seemed to be enjoying as Cassi so graciously helped him to remove his vest. Strapping herself into a window seat, Samantha didn't have quite as nauseating a view of Jack … and her.

"Would either of you like a drink?" Cassi asked, detaching herself from Jack.

The lighting certainly shined brightly enough in here. Samantha willed herself to keep her eyes on Cassi's face. "Not thirsty," she piped up between clenched teeth.

Jack ran his fingers through his hair, rearranging what Cassi had so conveniently left in disarray. "I'll have a double scotch, thanks."

"It's a shame Kevin couldn't join us. We could've had the best time. Where did he get off to, anyway?" Cassi dropped a couple of ice cubes in a glass and then poured the scotch over the ice.

"Back to New York for Evie's funeral." Samantha waited for Cassi's reaction.

Cassi chuckled. "Evie's funeral will be in New Orleans, of course. That's where she's from. Why I could even tell you the exact day she and Kevin met." Cassi handed the drink to Jack as the plane roared to life. "Don't worry about spilling it on takeoff. I can always get you another one." Her hand squeezed his bicep as she snuggled up next to him on the couch. "So what do you think of my mile high clubhouse?"

Jack wrapped his long fingers around the drink. "Samantha's a lot more than Kevin's new girlfriend. She's a hatchet man, and you know or at least you should that she would never tell you where Kevin is."

Cassi casually put her hand on Jack's knee, before turning to Samantha. "I think hatchet woman would be more appropriate. Anyway, I had to ask. I adore Kevin, and I hate it when one of my favorite boys is in trouble."

The plane lifted into the air and Samantha felt her blood pressure rising right along with it. *Her favorite boy. I could tell you the exact day Evie and Kevin met.* Being stuck in a tin can 7,000 feet in the air with the queen of porn made her want to gag. "Don't worry about me. I'll fix my own drink after all."

At least, the liquor cabinet brought a little comfort. Throwing in some ice along with pineapple and cranberry juice, she added the vodka and started sucking it down. Samantha slumped into her seat, trying to ignore Cassi rubbing up against Jack while she gave him a massage. The fact that Jack normally didn't wear tight fitting shirts but tonight sported a black t-shirt that clung to each one of his well-developed muscles didn't go unnoticed. He damn well better be enjoying this because she sure wasn't. But another drink might help.

Cassi rose from the couch and padded across the black shag carpet with bare feet. "Let's get this party started for real. I'll make each of us a round. Samantha, you're having a bay breeze right?"

Samantha handed her the empty glass and rolled her eyes at Jack.

"Don't take offense where Kevin is concerned. I wanted to talk to him tonight. The cops came up to my place today, asking a lot of questions. They said something about a murder investigation, and I don't think it involved Evie." Cassi handed Samantha her drink back and mixed one for herself.

Leaning back in her seat, Samantha took a sip. It most likely involved James. The cops had traced the car James was found in back to Kevin. So why did they go to Cassi for answers?

Taking Jack's empty glass, Cassi dropped an ice cube into it, which clinked when it hit the bottom. "I remember all too well when Kevin got sent to prison for killing Lexi."

Samantha's glass dropped from her hand. She barely caught it before it bounced off her lap and hit the floor. Brushing off the few drops that had splattered across her pants, she looked at Jack, whose jaw hung open.

"When was this?" Jack asked.

"Oh, maybe five years ago. I never thought Kevin did it, but Lexi drowned in Kevin's car. Supposedly, the two of them left a party after drinking too much, and Kevin drove off into a lake. Lexi never escaped her seatbelt. I refuse to believe the story myself."

"Lexi Hearn?" Alarms started ringing in Samantha's ears, but she couldn't quite remember why the name sounded familiar.

Jack's and Cassi's heads both snapped up at the same time. "That was her name," Cassi said, nodding her head vigorously, her big sea green eyes wide with sadness. "She used to work with me before Senator McCullen set her up in Florida. The next thing I knew she was dead and Kevin went to prison."

Cassi gulped down half of her drink, licking her bronze lips with her tongue. The only sound in the plane was the hum of the engine. Jack had taken to staring into his drink, and Samantha couldn't pull her eyes off of Cassi.

"I never thought he did it," Cassi continued in a small voice. She looked Samantha right in the eye. "Because I could've sworn I saw Kevin with Evie that night. But when I talked to Evie, she said I got my dates wrong." Cassi tapped her long french manicured fingernails on her glass. "It was right after the accident that Evie moved to New York because Kevin put her up in a penthouse there." Cassi finished her drink and shook her glass, letting the ice rattle. "I guess I need another one." She walked back over to the bar and began dropping more ice into her glass. "I don't get money wrong, and I don't get dates wrong." So how do you know Lexi Hearn?"

Samantha held the icy glass in her hand, not feeling the cold. She was numb as if stuck in a movie where reality doesn't exist, leaving only a part to play. The memories began folding in on her like a picture reel, clicking off footage: the funeral she had attended with Sam in Florida, the picture at Senator McCullen's house of him and Sam, Kevin telling her he had been in prison and Evie turning up dead.

It had been raining all day and everyone had big black umbrellas to keep their expensive clothes from getting wet. She remembered feeling so damp and out of place at the funeral. Sam had been vague about how he had known Lexi, but Samantha remembered meeting Senator McCullen—his southern accent and the way he had grasped Sam's arm when they shook hands, telling him everything would work out for the best. The picture she had seen at the senator's house flashed into her head. It had been taken the same day as the funeral because she remembered Sam had worn a grey dress shirt and black slacks. He had dressed up nicer on that day than he had for his own graduation.

Cassi took the drink out of Samantha's hand. "So how did you know Lexi?"

Samantha shook her head, trying to pull herself out of a bad dream. Her stomach had taken a free-for-all, and her heart felt like it would explode. She took a deep breath, trying to clear her head. "I didn't know her, but I went to her funeral in Florida."

Cassi stopped fixing Samantha's drink and looked at her. "I went to that funeral." She cocked her head from side to side, studying Samantha. "Who were you there with?"

And this is why she didn't talk about the past because it eventually brought up more questions. "I went with a guy I was dating at the time."

Cassi stirred Samantha's drink with a red stir stick and handed the bay breeze back to her. "Another thing I'm really good at is knowing when people lie to me, but I'm sure Jack would say you have your reasons for being dishonest."

Samantha took the drink and realized she wasn't pissed at Cassi anymore. "Maybe everyone is trying to stay alive."

Cassi smiled, a real genuine smile, which lit up her whole face. "Cheers to staying alive," she said as she toasted the air. Her long brown hair trailed down the front of her dress in big curls covering her breasts in a Lady Godiva sort of way. Green eyes twinkled in mischief as she tossed back a long sip of her drink.

"It's not a dragon on your ass; it's a panther, isn't it?" Samantha felt the words leaving her mouth but couldn't imagine how they had escaped her; except, of course, for the three or four drinks, she had consumed, which she had stopped counting or caring about.

Cassi beamed. "You're exactly right. It's a black panther. Do you want to see it? I love showing it off."

"Absolutely not," Samantha said, toasting the air with her own glass.

Chapter Fourteen

A slow constant pounding hammered in her head. Cotton mouth accompanied the head pounding, dragging her from unconscious to agonizing over waking up. Dimly, she became aware that her body lay wedged up against a very large, snoring man. Samantha scrunched her eyes closed tighter afraid of what she might find if she opened them. Her heart thumped in her chest, and she forced herself to open her eyes.

Dark curtains hung over the window, keeping any light from spilling in. Not daring to breath, she looked up to find Jack sound asleep. Her head rested on his arm, and his other arm wrapped around her, securing her to his chest. His black t-shirt molded nicely to his pecks, and stubble covered his jaw. With trepidation in her heart, she moved her gaze downwards. Oh, thank God. Her clothes along with Jack's remained intact.

She rolled to the side of the bed, dropped her feet to the floor and slowly inched the rest of herself off the bed, walking backwards until she made it into the bathroom and closed the door. With a heavy plump, she sat down on the toilet, put her head in her hands and tried to piece together last night's events. They had been on the plane, and she had downed too many drinks. Did she get in an argument with Cassi? She didn't remember. She thought Jack had carried her off the plane, and then they had talked, before going to sleep—but she couldn't really remember what about. Moisture beaded on her upper lip from the nausea that rolled around in her stomach.

"You don't have to hide in there all day," Jack yelled from the bedroom.

"I think it would be a good idea though." Samantha stood on shaking legs and splashed her face with cold water. After wiping her face with a brown hand towel, she dared to open the door.

Jack sat up in bed with his hair jutting out in different directions. "How are you feeling about things?"

"What things?" Samantha closed her eyes in concentration as if the events of last night would come back to her, but instead she remembered a lot of drinking and not much else.

Jack rubbed his jaw. "About Kevin killing Lexi Hearn?"

Oh, that was it. It felt like a sucker punch, knocking the wind out of her. She stumbled over to the bed and sat down. "I think I had blocked that out."

"Well, time to unblock and get on with our day."

"Why? Do you have a plan?"

"Same plan we had coming here—find Becki and take care of business. I'm going to take a shower." Jack stuck out his hand and ruffled Samantha's hair as he walked by.

She glanced around the room, trying to put together the blur of the night before. Polished wood floors gleamed against white walls. One yellow antique dresser with intricate flowers painted on each drawer stood against the wall. The brass headboard curved in swirls above the quilted floral bedcover—very homey.

Cassi pushed open the door and sauntered in, wearing a dusty rose negligee with a matching robe that didn't really cover anything. "I thought you might be up, and I brought you and Jack some drinks to ease you into the morning.

"I don't think my system can take anymore alcohol."

Setting one of the drinks on the dresser, Cassi shot Samantha a sideways grin and handed her the other glass. "I thought about adding liquor, but I knew you would turn it down."

Samantha's eyes narrowed at Cassi. "You don't make much sense."

"Don't I though?" Cassi beamed a giant smile, showing off perfectly whitened teeth as Jack opened the door to the bathroom, wearing only a towel. She spun around and took the glass of fresh squeezed juice to him. "I wanted to give you a good morning kiss." She stood on her tiptoes and gave him a kiss on the cheek.

Samantha groaned, grabbed her bag off the floor and skirted around Jack, pretending not to notice his newfound parasite. She locked herself in the bathroom and began taking off yesterday's clothes. Cassi's peals of laughter sent electrical shocks up Samantha's spine until it felt like her head might explode. Why did Cassi bother her so much? Shouldn't she be happy that someone liked Jack? Obviously, women found Jack attractive; of course, girls would be into him. A vision of Jack getting married to Cassi wearing a see-through wedding gown popped into her head. No, he couldn't be serious about her. Samantha flipped on the water happy to drown out Cassi's giggles.

After her shower, she quickly towel-dried her short hair and ran a comb through it. Dressing in a black silk top and black slacks, she breathed in deeply as she strapped her holster on and felt the heavy security of the gun against her ribs. Once she had her black suit jacket on, the reflection in the mirror made her laugh. Maybe she should rub a little war paint on her face to complete the picture.

"O.K., I'm coming out now." A prickling sensation of either fear or anxiety washed through her as her hand turned the knob on the door. The thought of finding Jack and Cassi in some lewd position on the bed hurt her stomach, but the room was empty. Samantha stood frozen in the doorway. Her heart pounded in her head. Wiping her free hand on her pants, she tossed her bag on the floor and stomped out of the room into a hallway with a large picturesque window at the end of it. The view revealed a wooden porch surrounded by a lush garden. At the far edge of the grounds, Samantha could see dense cyprus trees forming a wall between the well-kept garden and the rest of Louisiana.

Her footsteps echoed on the wood floor as she passed by numerous doors; until at the end of the hall, a large entrance opened into a living room. Every piece of furniture in the room displayed a different animal print. A zebra chair and matching footstool, a black and white cowhide covered couch and an overstuffed, brown chair with an unidentifiable hide surrounded a large fireplace. A picture of a naked lady stroking a leopard hung on the far wall. Samantha refused to let the picture creep her out even though the black eyes of the woman appeared to leer at her. She could barely jerk her attention away from the decor to spot Jack sitting at the bar with Cassi.

Jack turned around on his barstool, raised his eyebrow at Samantha and swiveled back around. "Cassi is making me another one of those amazing drinks. You want one?"

"No, I want to get going."

"My doesn't someone have murder in her eyes," Cassi purred.

"I'll be outside waiting for you," Samantha snapped. She couldn't take any more comments from people wearing negligees. Wandering off to the left past the bar, she heard Cassi call after her.

"The other way."

Samantha stopped and turned, slowly taking in Cassi's french manicured nail pointing at the doorway across the living room. Marching past both of them, she ignored Cassi's broad smile.

Her stride faltered as she entered the next room. The only light came from the sunlight spilling in from the opposite doorway. Cautiously, she stole through the more modern style entertainment area complete with a large screen T.V. and black leather furniture. The animal theme still carried over with an enormous zebra rug taking up the middle of the floor. An urge to draw her gun crossed her mind, but even the dark corners of the room appeared empty. The fact that Becki wanted her dead did nothing to calm Samantha's already shot nerves.

Stepping out of the dark room, Samantha blinked in the bright sunlight shining down from high rectangular windows. Spiral staircases wound upward, one on each side of the room, and two more entertaining rooms opened up from the foyer. Samantha couldn't resist snooping. How many chances would she get to check out a whorehouse? Antique furniture with dark wood and rose upholstery dominated the first room. Not exactly what she had expected. The other room showed off beach decor with glass french doors, leading out to a pool area.

"I thought you were pissed and leaving."

Samantha jumped when Jack's voice boomed behind her. "Pissed but curious." She shrugged her shoulders as she looked up to meet his warm brown eyes. The sunlight glowed around his brownish-blonde hair, which stuck straight up. His eyebrows arched perfectly over his eyes as he smirked in a way that irritated and inspired. Samantha paused for a moment, frozen in time, as her brain hijacked her emotions. Did she really not like Cassi, or did she not like Cassi liking Jack?

"Come on, let's get out of here." Jack opened the door and stepped out onto the porch.

Huffing and rolling her eyes, Samantha followed. Only when she stepped outside, did the reality of winter hit her. A cold breeze blew across the screened in wood porch, causing her to shiver. The dark wood sparkled as if the merry maids had recently finished dancing their way across it. It really didn't seem like a typical cathouse. Of course, Samantha didn't have much to compare it to other than the strip club where she had served drinks. This place definitely raised the bar. "So how did Cassi become the madam of a cathouse?"

Jack laughed, leading the way around the side of the house. "Her grandfather owned it. When he passed away, he left it to Cassi and Cynthia. But by that time, Cynthia was already dating some senator and didn't want anything to do with it. So, she turned it all over to Cassi."

The grounds boasted meandering paths that wound behind willowy trees and flowering bushes until Samantha could no longer see the paths. A huge, two-story, blue barn loomed in front of them. The oversized doors hung open, revealing a garage in the front part of the barn and a living room and bar area in the back.

"I came to a party here last spring. Talk about outstanding. Of course, if you think the way Cassi acts around me is annoying, you should see her around Kevin." Jack strode in and turned left, hitting an alarm button for a white sports car. "Cassi set us up with some nice wheels." Jack beamed as he opened the driver's side door.

Samantha ground her teeth. She needed Kevin to put some perspective on things. Is this what Kevin had meant when he said he hoped he didn't regret this? Samantha slid into the passenger's seat and strapped her belt on. "Where are we going?"

"I thought you wanted to track down Becki?"

"Sure," Samantha said, checking out her rear view mirror. The grounds remained completely empty. No one decided to follow them or, for that matter, get out of bed.

Beautiful grassy meadows sprang up along the way only to be hidden again by groves of trees. Maybe if Samantha could talk to Senator McCullen, he could clear up some of her doubt. He had been at the funeral in Florida. Why did that matter? Didn't she want to talk to Kevin, instead of digging for dirt on something that happened years ago? Her stomach rolled with a sour nauseous feeling.

After five minutes of winding along the country road, they finally hit the interstate. "How far from New Orleans is Cassi's place?"

"We have another 15 minutes before we're in town."

"Do you know Senator McCullen?"

Jack laughed and flicked his cigarette out the window. "You've been running with a different crowd than I have. I don't know any senators."

Samantha rolled her eyes in frustration. Her mind raced to Mr. Thompson, but then she remembered she and Jack weren't to have any contact with him. "Do you have a plan about how to get Becki?"

The first drop of rain hit the windshield. Jack wagged his eyebrows up and down. "One thing is for sure, and that is Becki has weaknesses. She loves to gamble, and she loves to shop. And I'm guessing she's in mourning over Ani.

Ani—how could anyone mourn over him? Her mind flashed back to the day he had broken into her and her brother's apartment and filled Sam with lead. It felt like years ago instead of less than a month. At least, she didn't have nightmares anymore—waking up in a cold sweat, frantically searching to see if anyone had busted the door down, or not. She snorted to herself.

"What?" Jack asked.

Samantha shrugged.

"You don't think anyone could miss Ani do you? That will get you killed. People in this business love the bad guy as much they love the good guy—sometimes more."

"What? Is that rule seventeen for your Hitman's Creedo?"

"Ha, rule seventeen states that when in New Orleans you should eat a muffuletta."

"I knew that," Samantha snapped.

Jack rolled his eyes and exited the freeway.

Chapter Fifteen

The smell of freshly baked bread filled the car, teasing Samantha, as she and Jack waited for the streetcar to pass. While they cruised slowly into the Garden District, she kept her eyes peeled, checking out each house. A solitary car crept down the street, splashing water from the quickly filling puddles. The fast moving storm kept most people at home, but Samantha still couldn't keep her head from spinning with all the beautiful houses to look at. Each one demanding her attention with their perfectly manicured gardens, wrought iron fences, balconies and huge fountains. The rain only added to their grandeur.

"That's it," Jack said, pointing to the right with his thumb.

Samantha craned her neck to get a good view of the half-hidden estate. It sat back on the lot, surrounded by large trees. One ancient live oak draped in spanish moss dwarfed all the others and looked to have been cut out of a gothic coloring book. During the month of December, when she lived here, the Garden District had been one of her favorite places to sightsee in New Orleans. Being strapped for cash at the time, anything inexpensive usually ranked high on the list of things to do. Not like window-shopping where the temptation to buy something depressed her.

Jack made a u-turn, positioning the car away from the direct line of view of the Guerrero household. The gated entrance exposed anyone entering or leaving the property.

Samantha tore into the brown paper bag with a vengeance. She handed Jack his muffuletta and smoothed the bag over her lap to avoid drips and keep the sandwich from burning her legs. "You really think she'll come out in this weather?" Samantha asked as a loud crack of thunder reverberated through the car.

"Don't know."

Samantha removed the paper from the sandwich and sunk her teeth into the genoa, cappicola, provolone, olive and caper masterpiece. She smiled, closing her eyes and letting the flavor fill her mouth.

"I haven't seen you this happy in a while," Jack said through a mouth full of muffuletta.

"I have a lot to be happy about. My boyfriend is possibly a psychotic killer, my partner is hooking up with a nudist/madam and I'm enjoying the perfect sandwich in a rain storm."

"So, basically it's just the sandwich."

"Exactly. Sam and I used to get these at least once a week."

They ate in silence. Samantha remembered how much Sam loved a muffuletta. He ranted and raved that Marcus made the only true muffuletta. She watched a cypress sway from a gust of wind. So easy peasy—the solution to finding Sam turned out to be right in front of her. If Sam still lived, all she needed to do was stake out Marcus's and badabing badaboom.

"Let's hit it." Jack started the engine and jerked the car into motion, sloshing Samantha's coffee before she had time to put anything away.

"Is it Becki?" Samantha scrunched her eyes, trying to get a better view of the limo that pulled out into the street and took off.

"No way of knowing," Jack said out of the corner of his mouth as he kept the other half of his cigarette firmly clamped between his lips.

It really seemed like quite the accomplishment to smoke, talk and tail someone at the same time. Of course, Jack appeared to be able to do all that and much more if need be. Samantha stuffed the rest of her sandwich back into the paper bag and unclipped her phone from her pants to put it on silence. No reason not to be prepared. But to her surprise, the phone was already set on silent, and she had a message. "Hey did you do this?"

"Do what?"

"Set my phone to silent."

Jack blew cigarette smoke out the cracked window as he flipped on the heater to keep the windows from fogging up. "Yeah, your phone became obnoxious last night. I finally got it to shut up."

"You should've answered it."

"I'm not playing cupid here, and if my phone goes off, I don't want you putting your paws on it."

"The next chance I get I will."

Jack glared at her and whipped the car into the next lane fast enough to make her slam against the door. Samantha ignored him. Her heart fluttered as she held the phone up to her ear to listen to the message.

"Hi, baby. I'm not having a good morning here. I couldn't get a hold of you, so I called Brody. Guess what. He says you and Jack are long gone. I'm dying to hear from you."

Suddenly, Samantha put the phone down, searching for a reason to explain her uneasiness. The black limo remained two cars ahead of them. Rain splattered on the windshield as the wipers swished back and forth. A pedestrian ran across the road, barely avoiding getting hit by a car, but Samantha felt a thousand miles away as if she was catching a glimpse of the scene through a looking glass.

The bullet hit the windshield in front of her. She sucked in a breath and glanced down at her clothes, expecting to find blood. The material looked perfect—not even a wrinkle on it. Samantha snapped her head back up to look at the windshield again, and then everything came into focus. The bullet had exited the windshield, and Jack was driving the car straight into a house.

Her mind spun in the obvious direction. Before she managed to turn her head, Samantha knew Jack had been hit. His head slumped towards her, and the blood ran down his black hunting vest. The car hit the corner of the house, exploding the air bags.

Even in a semi-conscious state, the panic set in immediately. Jack needed her. The back of her head hit the headrest, and her fingers clawed for the door handle. Fumbling around the airbag, it took several attempts to find the latch before the door flew open. She tried to jump out of the car, but her seat belt held her in place. Groping for the release, Samantha knew she and Jack were headed for either the gallows or the morgue. A sob tore from her throat before she could get the seat belt off of her. Finally, she half-stepped, half-fell out of the car.

A woman rushed out of the small house that now had part of a car sticking out of it. "I'm calling 911. Is anyone hurt?"

Samantha stumbled around the back of the car, holding on to it for support. The rain pelted down on her face, and her legs shook as she wrenched the door to the driver's side of the car open. The airbag completely covered Jack's face, revealing only a few rivulets of blood. Reaching into her boot, she pulled out her knife.

The woman on the phone screamed, "She has a knife."

A guy, who had been standing back with a small group of people on the sidewalk, jumped forward.

Ignoring the commotion, Samantha inserted the knife into the airbag. The stranger and she stood motionless, watching the bag wither from Jack's face. Samantha caught Jack's head before it fell forward. The bullet wound was on the side of the neck, but it looked like there had been a lot of blood loss. "Give me your shirt," she croaked.

With one quick tug, the guy next to her pulled a sweatshirt over his head and held it out to her.

"Wrap it around his neck, but don't choke him." She kept her hand on Jack's forehead. He hadn't moved. Samantha couldn't be sure, but she thought his breathing remained semi-normal. The sound of sirens ripped through the air.

The stranger tied the sweatshirt carefully around Jack's neck and looked right into Samantha's eyes.

In that brief second, Samantha's stomach did a free for all. The guy looked right at her, and if she could describe him, then he would be able to identify her. "Hold his head and put pressure on his neck." She let go of Jack's head when the guy replaced the hold with his hand. She cursed under her breath as the sound of the siren wailed again. Slipping her hand into Jack's jacket, she pulled out the guns one at a time. Samantha moved with her back to the small crowd, keeping the guns and knife between her and the car. She didn't bother to glance back at the guy holding Jack's head. Of course, he would describe her to the cops, but if she could get away for now that would be a huge help. Her ears strained, trying to listen to the three or four people gathered on the sidewalk, hoping no one would attempt to stop her.

"Move back and make room for the ambulance," yelled the woman who had called 911.

No one said anything as Samantha walked behind the car and then kept right on walking. She followed the side of the white clapboard house until she rounded the corner. Her legs wanted to crumple, but she willed herself to remain standing. The ambulance arrived with a last resounding wail of the siren and the slamming of doors. Her heart raced as she struggled to remain calm. She needed to escape without drawing more attention to herself. A feeling of déjà vu swept over her, followed by a bitter laugh. This wasn't déjà vu—she had done this before. A little more than two weeks ago, she had ended up in an alley in New Orleans, trying to shove a revolver down her pants so no one would see it.

Laying the guns on the ground, her hands began to shake. She tucked her knife into her boot, taking a deep breath when her fingers kept fumbling with the leg of her pants. Then picking the guns up, Samantha shoved one halfway down on each side of her pants. At least today, she had a jacket.

Directly in front of her, a path meandered between the backyards of shotgun houses. Walking as fast as she dared, she concentrated on keeping her thoughts rational. Fear gnawed at her. Someone could be tracking her. Stopping in the middle of the path, Samantha looked back, making sure that no one had followed her. The cold rain kept the nausea at bay. How was she going to check on Jack? She sent a silent prayer that Jack would stay alive and need someone to check on him.

The sirens started up again, and Samantha tripped in a puddle. An intersection loomed maybe a quarter of a mile away. She would definitely have to cross the street eventually. Pausing for a moment, random thoughts flashed in her head. She couldn't see the house she and Jack had run into because the path, thankfully, had made too many twists. There was absolutely no one to call, but the thought of getting a room near Marcus's Muffuletta Shop seemed like a perfect solution. Not wanting to reach the intersection too soon in case the cops were already looking for her, she slowed her pace, letting the rain run down her face unheeded.

Maybe she should be grateful for the rain. At least, there weren't very many pedestrians out, walking in the storm. The sound of sirens grew distant and no longer gave her heart palpitations. She couldn't figure out why the cops hadn't started chasing her by now, but whatever the reason, she felt relieved. Probably taking Jack's guns wasn't the smartest move.

The thunder boomed as lightning streaked across the sky. By the time she made it across the street, her clothes hung off of her and dripped with water. She pulled her jacket out in front of her to keep it from clinging to the guns. Earl Street was a long line of businesses on both sides of the road. To Samantha's relief, they didn't have glass storefronts. A door to a pool hall opened, and a woman stepped out with enough makeup on to cover a baboon's ass. She lit a cigarette and let it dangle while her eyes followed Samantha as she passed by. Samantha walked even faster determined to keep her teeth from chattering.

Chapter Sixteen

The rain dripped off her nose as she pushed the door open to the hotel. The place was small and far from posh but offered something even better—relief from the storm. The elderly desk clerk looked up from his novel 'Hatchet Man,' raised his eyebrows and proceeded to mark his page with an air of disapproval. Samantha snorted. Maybe someone should write a book about her and call it 'Hatchet Woman.'

She tried not to shake herself like a wet dog, but water trickled down her back, making her jerk. As indiscreetly as possible, she pulled a hundred dollar bill out of her pants pocket. "Do you have a room?"

"Sure, eighty a night."

Samantha trudged across the linoleum floor and held out the wet bill. Her left hand remained on her jacket, holding it closed and keeping it pulled out as far away from her as possible.

"I need an ID."

Putting her hand back into her pocket, she fished around until she could extricate the driver's license without having the wad of bills fall on the floor. Granted she had grabbed only a thousand this morning more because she didn't trust Cassi than anything else.

The guy nodded as he took the license and finger pecked the information into the computer.

Wide, brown, diamond-shaped keys hung on a rack behind the grey-haired clerk's head, suggesting an era older than Samantha's. Empty brown mail slots waited for post, they probably hadn't received in twenty years. A sitting room took up a corner of the lobby complete with large windows, which looked out at the falling rain and empty streets.

"Quite a storm out there," he said, pushing the room key, change and driver's license across the short counter towards her. "Second door on the left as you go up the stairs. Enjoy your stay, Miss Cross."

Samantha grimaced and sloshed her way across the lobby. She couldn't control the chill that made her whole body shake. At the top of the stairs, Samantha breathed out a sigh of relief; there was no one around. In fact the only sound came from the clerk downstairs. Taking advantage of the empty hallway, she let go of her jacket, stopped in front of room number three, slid the key into the lock and opened the door.

The door closed behind her with a solid click. Quickly locking the door and fastening the chain into place, she slumped against the wall, thankful, to rest her shaking legs. The memory of Jack's pale and clammy head in her hand made her sick. Who would check on him? Whom could she call? She didn't have Bruno's number, couldn't call Mr. Thompson and didn't trust Cassi. Kevin could help maybe, but she didn't have his number either. Her eyes closed for a minute. Weariness set in like an oppressive weight tied around her neck.

Pushing off from the wall, she shook all the way to the tiny bathroom. The possibility of shock entered her mind, but most likely the freezing rain had taken its toll. Samantha stripped her jacket off and spread a towel out on the floor, very carefully laying the guns down and drying them off. Adding her knife to the pile, she wiped it, too. Finally, with frozen fingers, she removed her wet clothes and climbed into the shower. The hot water pelted her, slowly thawing her numb body.

Samantha jerked open the shower curtain, realizing a little too late the bathroom had turned into a steam room. Just what the guns needed more moisture. She toweled off her red skin and wrapped a towel around herself. Grabbing the phone off the counter, she sat down on the toilet. Fantastic, she had missed a call from Kevin because her stupid ringer was off. Holding her head in her hand, she groaned out loud.

After hanging up her wet clothes and tucking the two extra guns under the mattress, Samantha crawled into bed.

The ringer on her cell phone was turned up as loud as it would go, and she carefully situated the phone on the pillow beside her head with a gun hidden underneath. The rain drizzled outside her window as she snuggled under the crisp, clean bedding for warmth. The clothes hung above the heater blocking part of her view, but she knew the rain wasn't stopping for a while. Her mind reeled around all the scenarios of how she could get to Jack, but they all ended with her getting caught and sitting in a slammer.

The real question was who had shot Jack, and more importantly how easy it had been. The shot had come from somewhere other than the limo—she knew that. Had Cassi tipped someone off? The rain pelted on the window as Samantha's head swirled with all the same thoughts she had considered on the long walk here. The heaviness of her eyelids won out, leaving her caught in a web of nightmares. This time she didn't hear the splintering of the door when he kicked it in. His shoes made no noise as he walked into the room and came to stand over her bed. In her mind, she woke up, staring at the barrel of Ani's gun and his black eyes, which boiled with a hate death hadn't tamed.

The sharp ring of the phone brought her straight up in bed. The dark room pressed down on her, making it hard to focus. Her heart hammered in her chest. It took a couple of rings for her to realize the sound came from a phone instead of a gun going off. Picking up the phone, she mumbled, "Hello." Kevin's voice replaced her panic with relief.

"You're really pissing me off. Why don't you answer your phone?"

Memories of the accident flooded through her, and she held her breath, despising the tear that slid down her cheek. "Jack got shot, and I can't go to the hospital to check on him because I know they'll identify me."

"Did you call the hospital?"

The calmness in his voice gave Samantha hope. "No, I…." She stopped a sob before it could escape.

"Are you hurt?"

"No."

"Which hospital is he at?"

"I don't know," Samantha wailed.

"Take deep breaths. I'm going to track down where he's at, and I'll call you back. Can you stay by the phone?"

"Yes." She whispered, wanting nothing more than Kevin to be here, holding her. She clicked the phone off. What a wimp, and she hadn't even thought to call the hospital. The quiet darkness of the room sank deep into her bones. No sounds came from any of the other rooms. Did this place even have other guests? She felt safe here, but the idea scared her. Safe didn't usually last long. Unconsciously, she stuck her hand under the pillow, wrapping her fingers around her gun. Cold steel couldn't replace her need for Kevin.

Needing Kevin—her thoughts ricocheted around in her head. She didn't want to need him. She didn't want to need anyone. Attachments made things painful. Closing her eyes, she tried to squeeze out the panic that too much thinking brought on. A boiling sensation started in her stomach and then rolled upwards. She swung her legs off the bed, feeling the cool floor beneath her feet. Now wasn't the time to lose her head.

Samantha left her gun on the end of the bed, wrapping a towel around her as she went to the window. The clothes felt warm and crisp to the touch. The old-fashioned heater with its wide metal bars and gaps left her with a newfound respect for it. This was no clunky piece of steel—this baby had power. Outside the window the rain had stopped, but the late afternoon looked gloomy with dark clouds floating low above the city. The smell of fresh rain through the window offered an appeal that the early darkness lacked.

Deciding against the peep show, Samantha took her clothes into the bathroom. As she pulled the rumpled suit on, it became obvious she needed a disguise because without a doubt the guy at the wreck had blabbed everything to the police. Unlike Jack, Samantha lacked the nerve to turn on the news. The thought of the police looking for her caused an unpleasant sensation to settle in her stomach. Her nerves didn't need the extra jolting that seeing her face plastered on the T.V. would give her.

With shaky fingers, she tried smoothing her suit into place. The reflection in the mirror revealed blue eyes jumping out from a pale face. Her short blonde hair swung to the side. How much of her appearance would she have to change? Two weeks ago long blonde hair had hung past her shoulders; now it barely hit below her chin. She closed her eyes and gripped the sink. It would be all right. Everything would work out, one way or another.

Methodically securing her knife in her boot, she holstered a gun. The wad of money felt comforting in her pocket, but eventually she would need more cash. Kevin would help her. It dawned on her that for the first time in a long time she felt a sense of security, but the feeling came from knowing that Kevin and Jack would take care of her. Once upon a time she had believed her brother would take care of her. Without a doubt, taking care of herself eliminated disappointment.

The door made a small squeak as she pushed it open into the hall. Not even a dust particle bothered to float through the air as she made her way to the stairs and began to descend downward. She reached the third to the last step when her heart completely stopped.

He sat nonchalantly in a large floral chair with one leg crossed over the other as he held a magazine in his lap. He was tall. She remembered that from the car accident. When he had helped her with Jack, she had only come up to his shoulders. He wore the same clothes: a yellow t-shirt and gray sweat pants. Friendly green eyes locked onto her, followed by a grin that was too large—it matched all his features, including his brown hair that waved slightly out of place. He looked like a P.E. instructor, but he wasn't here to recruit her for a volleyball game.

The option to run crossed her mind. Her cell phone rang, breaking the crackling silence as she stood frozen on the stairs, trying to decide if she should continue forward or retreat rapidly.

"You should answer that." His voice held a note of concern, comforting—like a father giving his daughter some good advice.

Samantha ignored the phone. Taking the creaky stairs slowly, she came to stand in front of him, before moving to the side of the stairs and sitting on a matching floral settee directly across from him.

"I didn't mean to scare you," he said, placing the magazine on the table beside him and leaning forward.

"I don't scare easily." Samantha felt certain he was unarmed, but somehow he had followed her here— without her knowing.

"From an outsider's point of view it seems you haven't made friends with the Guerreros."

"Who are they?" She batted her eyes, hoping the dumb blonde routine worked on him.

He chuckled and leaned back in his chair. "They're the ones I watch as I jog past their house in an attempt to keep an eye on them. I was giving up today because of the storm, heading back to my car when the limo passed me. So I stopped to see which way it was going, and that's when I heard the shot."

Cop, Cop, Cop! Why else would he stake out the Guerreros? "So did you see who shot us?"

He shrugged his broad angular shoulders. "I saw a tan sedan accelerate right after the shooting. I didn't see who was in the car, but I know who usually drives that car."

"Aren't you a helpful little birdie."

The cop's face split between a lopsided grin and eyes that looked down his long nose with the intensity of a hawk. "I thought a little helpful information might make this easier."

Samantha's stomach rolled with unease. What a crappy day. "This?" She arched her eyebrow and pursed her lips.

"I need some info."

Samantha shrugged. Her eyes wandered to the door and back to the guy in front of her. She could disappear again, but this guy had found her without any backup. So he was either really good (that would be bad) or he was really desperate (a little better, but then prone to act on God only knew what).

He grinned again, and this time it lit up his whole face. Samantha knew that grin. It made her stomach cramp and her head scramble. It said go ahead because you're not going to get very far at all.

Chapter Seventeen

Samantha drummed her fingers on her pants leg. Focusing on breathing, she took one long breath and then another. "What do you want?" her voice broke the silence.

"I'm one of the best trackers in the world, but every once in a while, someone that I have an interest in disappears." He leaned forward, putting his face a sparse twelve inches from Samantha's face. The smell of strawberry shampoo hung in the air between them. "I want Kevin Jacobs."

He might as well have hit her in the chest with a sandbag. "Why?" The word sprang out of her mouth before she could reel it back in.

He frowned as if the whole affair saddened him. "I keep track of him, and now he's gone."

Samantha's phone rang. A bead of sweat started at her hairline and began to trickle down her face by her ear. "I got that ace, but why do you keep track of him?" Another ring screamed through the silence. Samantha rolled her eyes. "It's my boyfriend. He wants to know where I'm at all the time."

"Then you should answer it and tell Kevin you're here with me."

Her blue eyes held his green ones and it was obvious neither one of them would give.

"No problem," he said standing. "You don't have to tell me a thing. I'll follow you, and you'll take me right to him."

Samantha watched him turn and leave. The sound of his tennis shoes squeaking on the floor echoed in the silence until he opened the door, and the noise of the street filtered in. And then the silence returned. She had major problems now.

Her phone rang again, sounding like an angry hornet that wouldn't quit buzzing. Her hand shook from nerves as she fished the phone from the clip on her pants. How could she answer it here? He probably bugged the whole place. Oh, screw it.

"What do you want?" She snapped into the phone as she headed outside. He couldn't have bugged anything outside the hotel. So, O.K., let him follow her. She didn't even know where she was going.

"Wow, talk about personality disorder," Kevin said. I didn't know you had so many sides."

"It's been that kind of day. When it's bad, it gets worse."

"What's wrong now?"

"Oh, you know. I now have a police stalker who is convinced I know some idiot named Kevin something or other, and he says he'll follow me until he finds Kevin." She marched blindly along the street, plowing down the wet sidewalk in no particular direction. Not bothering to pay attention if anyone followed her or not, she needed to walk and think.

"It's O.K. You're going to be fine. Good news. Looks like your friend made it through surgery. He's in recovery at St. Vincent's. You don't need to do anything, but come and see me."

She stopped cold in the street. A guy behind her bumped into her, and she spun around, knowing it had to be the cop. It wasn't. An older man shook his head at her and moved on.

"I just told you," her voice cracked with frustration.

"I heard exactly what you said. I'm going to help you. Remember where we were when I told you I was on parole."

Samantha shook her head, realizing it was really cold outside, and her fingers were starting to turn blue.

"Go there, but instead end up where we had first arrived in town. You're looking for Pussy."

It sprang out of her unbidden. A sudden peel of laughter lighting up her insides as she stood in the gloomy street next to a shop that displayed casual dresses. The dress that stood out in the window reminded her of a romantic getaway on a private beach. It looked light and silky as if even in this dreary weather, spring might break through. Her fingers were completely frozen, and she had started to shake. "Can I buy a dress before I go looking for pussy?"

"Absolutely, but don't go back to anywhere you've been."

"But ..."

"No, I told you what to do. Buy your dress and come to me. It shouldn't take you more than an hour."

Her voice got stuck in her throat. "Sure," she whispered. Clicking the phone off, she felt her whole body sag with relief and apprehension. She could do this. Jack was going to make it. Kevin had ditched this guy before; he knew how to handle this.

Pushing on the door, the heat from the dress shop rushed to meet her along with the smell of honeysuckle.

The lady behind the counter looked up from a stack of receipts. "It's quiet today. I ended up getting my paperwork out to keep me busy."

"No problem, I got caught in the rain earlier and need a few things." Samantha almost screamed with excitement. Behind the counter next to the wall of shoes were wigs: blonde, red and brunette. For the first time, since she had encountered the volleyball coach, she felt hopeful.

Casually walking towards the rack of dresses, which had caught her eye in the street, Samantha found her size.

She kept it positioned away from the windows, so no one from outside could see what she had picked out. "If you don't mind, I'm going to need a little help."

The clerk's head popped up, sending her long grey hair flying. Her sparkly red earrings bobbed with enthusiasm. "Of course."

Samantha exhaled. "I have a stalker."

The smile disappeared on the woman's face as she pressed her lips together.

"It is very important my purchases are concealed, so he will have a harder time spotting me. I want this dress and the medium length brunette wig—the one that's tapered around the face. Also a pair of shoes to match the dress in a size 9 would be great."

Stepping from behind the counter, the clerk took the dress and very discreetly disappeared into the back. "I'll get the merchandise packaged back here. You might take a look at our jackets. The forecast for the rest of the week is not very good, I'm afraid."

Samantha spotted it before the words were out of the clerk's mouth. A brilliant blue trench coat complete with shimmering jewel stone buttons jumped out at her. Would the jacket be peacocking, or was it so opposite of what she wore that he would be fooled? Feeling the thick wool won her over; no one would be able to see the bulge from her gun.

Again Samantha turned in an effort to hide the coat. She approached the counter and waited as the clerk finally returned from behind the curtain.

"Everything is in the bag. Oh, I see—that's a beautiful choice." Taking the coat, she arranged it in the bag behind the counter. "Let's see now." Tapping the amount into the cash register, she smiled. "Your total comes to $546.98."

Samantha grimaced. If she had to buy a plane ticket, her life was in the crapper, but remembering the last time she escaped from New Orleans, this trip paled in comparison. Maybe she shouldn't come back here. It felt like every time she got inside the city limits all hell broke loose. "If anyone asks what I purchased, could you give them some false information?"

"Don't worry, dear. That is exactly what I'll do." She gave her the change and patted her hand.

Samantha smiled to herself. Not everyone in New Orleans wanted her head on a stick, maybe just the majority. As she pushed open the door and stepped out onto the sidewalk, a gust of freezing cold wind knocked the air out of her. Absently wiping her tearing eyes with her jacket sleeve, Samantha watched a stream of cars whizz by, splashing muddy water onto the sidewalk. She couldn't see the cop in the yellow t-shirt, but she had a feeling he knew how to follow without being seen. Acting on instinct, Samantha used her one free arm to hail a cab. It rolled to a stop, and she climbed in.

"Where to Miss," the cabby asked, not bothering to turn around.

"Take me to the.... No, how about Marcus's Muffuletta Shop."

"Yeah, this kind of weather makes you want a nice, hot sandwich doesn't it?"

Samantha nodded, searching the storefronts for any sign of her newfound friend. He might still be standing outside in the cold, waiting to follow her, or maybe he hailed a cab to catch up. Quite possibly, the whole New Orleans' Police Department was on her tail. Well, she would find out soon enough.

Paying the cabby, she jumped out of the taxi and made her way into Marcus's. Only a few customers sat around the bright yellow tables. Even the weather, couldn't keep the die-hards from having their muffuletta. She made her way to the counter, recognizing the owner from the numerous trips her brother and her had made to this restaurant. "I'll take an original. You haven't seen my brother drop by today have you?"

Marcus looked up from behind the glass counter. "I almost didn't recognize you with that hair cut. Where you been? Your brother said you were out of town."

Adrenaline raced through her, making Samantha's heart pound in her chest. She knew it. That rotten, no good for nothing, lying, cheating, conniving psychopath was still alive. Instantly, she felt relieved and pissed all at the same time. Her throat closed up as she fought back the tears. "I'm going to give you my new phone number. If you could pass it on to him, I'd appreciate it."

Marcus spread the olives on the sandwich. "Write it on the back of that business card, and I'll pass it on to him."

Scribbling her new number on the card, anger flashed through her as her fingers shook. Couldn't he have let her know he was alive by now? Why this stupid cat and mouse game? She absently paid for the sandwich and walked out of the shop, clutching the bag to her chest. The warmth of the sandwich seeped through her thin shirt, but she had become oblivious to the cold. Catching a different taxi, she didn't notice if anyone stood in a corner watching her. Leaves and trash danced down the street, caught in the cold wind.

Inside the cab, she slumped in the seat. Finally, the taxi driver's voice rose loud enough to penetrate through the fog.

"Where to?"

Samantha's head snapped up. The taxi driver had turned around in his seat to face her. His eyes were wide with his eyebrows arching up, waiting for her to answer.

"Take me to the Night Owl." If her brother still got sandwiches from Marcus's, why wouldn't he still hang out at the Night Owl?

Chapter Eighteen

Night came fast. As the cab pulled up to the Night Owl, the streetlights blinked on. The storm had skipped over dusk, and the darkness lay heavily on the empty street. Samantha closed the squeaking cab door, watching it drive away into the inky blackness along with any resemblance to rational thought. The same yellowed and peeling sign hung above the stairwell entrance. She descended the cement staircase slowly, not wanting to slip on the wet steps. A dim bulb above the door put off enough light that Samantha paused before touching the grubby doorknob.

There were groups of people scattered at different tables, and a few stragglers seated at the bar. But her brother was not among them. Why did she entertain the illusion that he would be here? Taking a back booth, she ordered a coffee when the waitress rushed past.

Carefully unwrapping her sandwich, Samantha resigned herself to living on muffulettas. Kevin was going to be mad she hadn't gone to the airport, but what good would it do him if she led the detective right to him. Biting into her sandwich, a fleeting moment of bliss passed over her before the waitress plopped the coffee down in front of her, sloshing the coffee onto the table.

"So, where's your brother tonight?"

Samantha recognized the brunette with the short curly hair from the few times she had come in with Sam. "Not here I guess."

"No, it's pretty early, but he'll probably show up around midnight. He loves to wait until everyone is drunk, and then he starts up a craps game in the backroom."

Samantha raised her eyebrows studying the girl's face. She looked barely twenty with big brown eyes to match her full lips. Samantha could easily see why Sam hung out here, having this pretty girl cater to him. Everyone liked to be treated special, and Sam knew exactly how to elicit that behavior from people—especially women. "Did he come in last night?"

She shook her head, sending her curls bouncing in different directions. "No, it's been a few nights."

"Hey, can we get some service over here." One of the guys from the bar yelled at the waitress as he clunked his empty beer on the counter.

She rolled her eyes and turned toward the customer.

Pictures of past Mardi Gras' queens decorated the wall. Samantha knew quite a few families put a lot of emphasis on being part of the New Orleans' traditions. Invitation-only krewes made up a lot of the parades and balls that occurred during the Mardi Gras' season. It did seem funny that a bar like this would keep up with New Orleans' high society.

She ate her sandwich slowly, savoring the combination of genoa, cappicola and olives, but she finally gave up on resisting the urge to look at all the pictures. Wrapping her sandwich back in the paper, she got up and started studying each photo, beginning at the back wall. Two booths down from where she began a feeling of ice-cold dread hit her. Becki Guerrero stood next to a throne, her face glowing as another young woman, who looked like a dead ringer for Lisa, placed a crown on Becki's head. Samantha's eyes snapped to the picture above where Lisa's lookalike received her crown, but the name on the picture was Lexi Hearn.

"Find anything important, or do you have a thing for Mardi Gras?"

Samantha jumped up from the booth she had leaned into only to come face to face with the detective from this afternoon. She stepped back, glowering at him. "I told you. I don't know where Kevin is."

"Lexi Hearn—now that's a name that hasn't come up in conversation for a long time."

Samantha narrowed her eyes at him and brushed past him to return to her seat. She plunked down, taking a sip of her cold coffee.

The detective slid into the seat across from her. His green eyes cut into her and locked on her gaze.

"What do you know about Lexi Hearn?" The cramping in her stomach from last night's conversation with Cassi and Jack came back.

The detective sat back against the faded red vinyl booth and clasped his hands in front of him on the table. "It made all the papers, you know. Notorious mobster's son kills debutante. You couldn't concoct a better story than that to sell papers. The press loved it. They dug into his family history and exposed every detail of his life. Kevin did hard time, and then one day when the press wasn't paying attention anymore, he walked.

"And that's when you started following him around?" Samantha took a sip of her coffee and let the last dreads of the cold tar run down the back of her throat. Her phone rang, breaking the staring contest between her and her new stocker. This time she snapped the phone open and snarled into it, "I can't go looking for pussy right now."

"I didn't know you spent your time looking for pussy, too."

She almost dropped the phone. The globed lights that hung from the ceiling swayed. "Where are you?" her voice came out in a rushed whisper.

"M.M.S."

"I'll be there in ten minutes." Samantha stood and her legs wobbled as if she was on a ship in the middle of a storm. The lights above her swung from side to side, pulsating with the blaring music, which all of a sudden made the inside of her head pound. He was alive. Sam was alive and waiting at Marcus's. All she had to do was get there.

Jerking the door to the street open, she hunched her shoulders against the cold wind. Two steps at a time she raced up the wet stairs, missed a step and fell forward. Her hands took the brunt of the fall, barely stopping her head from cracking on the cement. Samantha pushed herself up, brushed off her palms and shook them to block the pain. With a much slower gate, she grasped her bag and trod up the stairs.

The dark empty street completely lacked the remote possibility of a cab driving by.

"I can give you a ride."

Samantha spun around. This guy really annoyed her. She hadn't noticed him following her out of the bar. The phone call from Sam had sent all other thoughts out of her head. She bit her lip as she looked down the dreary street, hoping to see an illuminated sign on top of a taxi. A freezing cold gush of wind hit her, chilling her to the bone.

"Yeah, sure," Samantha grunted as she stood on the sidewalk with her shoulders hunched. He strode towards a small hatchback parked three spaces down. Why would she even consider getting a ride with this guy? Glancing behind her, she spotted an alley to her left. If she ran right now, she might be able to lose him. Another cold gust sucked her breath away, and then the car pulled up beside her. Oh, fine. She yanked open the door and folded herself into the passenger seat.

"Where are we going?"

"Marcus's Muffuletta Shop—you know where it is?"

"Of course, are you meeting Kevin?"

Samantha sighed. Her head spun in a thousand different directions at once. "You wish."

It didn't take long to get back to the muffuletta shop. The heater in the car felt good against her legs as the radio pumped out soft jazz. The cop did a u-turn so he could drop Samantha off right in front of the shop. She could see inside the large window that her brother wasn't there. Her hopes sunk. With great effort, she forced herself out of the car and lumbered into Marcus's.

Marcus smiled from behind the counter, shaking his head. "He took off one minute ago. But don't worry; he left this for you."

Samantha picked up the piece of crumpled paper with her heart pounding in her ears.

Don't trust Kevin and don't trust John.

She didn't know who John was, but she glanced out the window, thinking she could probably make a good guess.

The gunfire shattered the peacefulness of the restaurant and turned her stomach to water. Marcus ducked down behind the counter. Fear rolled through her, making it hard to think. She heard her phone ring, but ignored it as she staggered away from the counter, making her way to the back door. Zigzagging around customers that now lay on the floor, Samantha kept moving until she made it to the exit.

Outside the cold wind hit her almost as fast as the hand that snaked out of dark, grabbing hold of her flimsy jacket and pulling her to him. Her fist slammed into the large hulk holding her jacket when she felt a gun nozzle press against her back. Fingers wrapped in her hair, pulling her lower and closer to someone standing behind her. "You don't remember me, but I remember you."

The voice rasped with hate, but she had no idea who it was. The guy in front of her reached inside her jacket and took out her gun. He dropped it in the bag she had been carrying from the store and jerked it away from her. Fingers cinched even tighter in her hair, making her want to scream. Yes, she should scream. Opening her mouth, she barely got out a squeak before the guy in front of her shoved a large cloth over her mouth and nose.

Chapter Nineteen

The weight of her eyelids made her want to keep them closed. If only she could go back to sleep, but something didn't seem right. A part of her kept screaming, wanting her to open her eyes. With way more energy than she felt like exerting, Samantha managed to flutter them open briefly. The effort made her head swim, and she closed them again, trying to figure out why she needed to wake up. The dark room didn't offer a lot of clues. Maybe a light switch would help. She tried to lift one of her arms, but it wouldn't move. She tried the other arm, wondering why it felt so hard to do anything. Finally, she lifted a leg. Panic set in as she realized her hands were bound behind her head. The memory of a guy putting a cloth over her face surfaced from the dizziness. Who would want to abduct her? The man said he knew her, but how could that be possible?

Thoughts of Sam flitted through her head. Without a doubt, Samantha knew Sam didn't have a hand in this. Did he get shot moments before she ran out the back door? No, it had to have been the cop or someone else. Or she skipped out like the last time Sam got shot.

A bump from outside her door swung her mind back to the present. She wrenched open her eyes, willing herself to study the room. The window let in very little light. She narrowed her eyes not sure of her vision, but maybe in the corner of the room stood a camera on a tripod stand. Tasting bile at the back of her throat, she closed her eyes, trying to keep her fear from taking over. Now more than ever she needed a clear head.

The bump came again, but this time the door swung open.

She winced when someone clicked on the overhead light. The bright light burned her eyes, but even in the two seconds she fought to keep her eyes open, she recognized Becki Guerrero. Heels clacked across the floor as Becki approached the bed. In a desperate attempt to fight the lethargy, Samantha made out a vision of long dark hair and a sweater covered in gold chains.

"Don't worry, Samantha. I won't stay long. Pelo, oh, you remember him don't you?" Becki leaned over Samantha's face, leering. "You killed his friends Cano and Edwardo. Maybe you don't remember because of the trail of bodies you leave behind, but Pelo remembers." She tapped Samantha on the nose with one long red nail, before walking to the window where Samantha's bag sat. Picking it up by the twine straps, she turned back to Samantha.

"What Pelo's going to do to you, I don't want to be around for, but know this because I don't think you'll live through tonight. Jack will be dead before the night is over, and I promise you that I'll make Kevin's death as long and as painful as your own." She winked, holding up the bag. "Kevin put a tracker in your phone to keep tabs on you. It will be easy to catch him when he comes rushing to save you." Becki waved, before slithering out the door.

A dull rage swept over Samantha. She'd get out of this if for no other reason than to shoot Becki in the head. The rope cut into her wrists as she tried to loosen them, but surely this would be nothing compared to what Pelo planned to do. Pulling and twisting and picking at the knots with numb fingers didn't have any effect on the rope. A peal of laughter from outside her door caused another corkscrew of hate to spiral through her. Becki wouldn't be laughing forever.

Samantha stared at the door, trying to keep calm while each second ticked away. She looked at her boots still on her feet and began to writhe her foot out of the boot. It didn't take too long to get the foot free, but the hard part was going to be getting the knife. She managed to free the other foot and, using her toes, take off one of her socks.

How much time did she have left? Her brain screamed none as she fought against herself to stay focused. Her toes wrapped around the end of the knife, but it didn't want to pull free from the boot. She felt hotter and more panicky each time her toes slid off the knife. Exasperation set in when the knife slipped out of her grasp again. Four minutes, maybe five minutes had passed. Her heart pounded, making it hard to think. Her toes grabbed the knife, and this time it broke free from the sheath inside the boot. Carefully and slowly, she brought the knife up to her hands by lifting her legs over her head.

Her fingers grasped the blade, holding it laboriously to prevent it from dropping to the floor. Making small movements, she began to scrape at the rope. Without being able to see what she was doing, Samantha had to hope she would cut through the rope in time.

Footsteps in the hall caused her to stop moving. If someone came in, she wouldn't be able to hide the knife. Maybe if she put her feet back in her boots, they wouldn't notice. Sliding her feet back into her boots as best as she could, Samantha continued cutting at the rope. Her fingers began to cramp and burn. The pain shot down from her fingers into her arms, making her tremble from the effort.

The footsteps began again and this time stopped outside her door. Her heart pounded in her ears, but despite the fear, which chilled her to the bone, the door opened anyway.

Pelo swaggered into the room, cocking his head to level his malevolent gaze onto Samantha. She could feel the hate, which glittered in his dark eyes, boring into her. Feigning sleep, she recognized the guy behind him as the one who had jerked her to him and taken her gun when they had abducted her. He went straight to the camera, dragging it out of the corner and positioning it closer to the bed.

Pelo let out a wild laugh and strode over to Samantha, yanking the knife away from her. "Perfect," he hissed as he leaned close to her. "I don't have to worry about getting mine bloody." He licked her cheek slowly, his eyes burning with a feverish crazed look, before turning his attention to the camera guy. "You ready?" he asked, stalking away from the bed.

Samantha tugged even harder, trying to break the rope. A searing pain shot up her arm as she struggled to break free. Her head spun with dizziness, and a tear trickled down the side of her face.

The camera guy stood up from cleaning the lens. "I'll be in the hall if you need me."

"We won't," Pelo said and pulled his long sleeve shirt off over his head, revealing a torso covered in hair. He walked toward the bed, holding the knife; it glittered from the overhead bulb.

Samantha could smell him as he came closer. Fear replaced fatigue as the combination of his heavily spiced cologne mixed with rancid sweat reached her nose. Her mind raced, trying to decide if putting up a fight would be better than pretending to go along with the plan, but as Pelo closed in, she couldn't take it. The overwhelming smell of him, made her kick him as hard as she could in the chest.

He staggered back a few feet. "I knew you would be fun," he said, grinning as he lunged at her again. He ducked to the side of her kicking feet and landed on top of her.

Her right hand broke free of the rope, and she shot the palm of her hand into his nose. She had wanted to do it hard enough to drive the bone of his nose into his skull like Jack had showed her, but instead she had only managed to send him staggering backwards and shaking his head from side to side.

Pelo leaped towards her, growling and bringing the knife up to her throat. This time Samantha gouged her thumb into his eyeball. There was no mercy. She shoved her thumb as deep into his socket as she could.

Pelo crumbled to the floor.

Samantha grabbed the knife Pelo had dropped on the bed and began using it to saw away the rest of the rope from her other wrist. With both hands free at last, she gripped the blade so tightly her fingers turned white as she slid off the other side of the bed, keeping her eyes on Pelo. He didn't make a move. He lay on floor with his head in his hands and his legs tucked up in fetal position. Maybe he had passed out.

Her whole body shook from fear or rage or something so primal she couldn't name it. Samantha shoved her feet all the way into her boots and wobbled towards the door. Keeping the knife by her side, she cracked open the door, cringing at what she might find. The hall appeared to be as empty as a confessional on a Saturday night. She cautiously moved in the direction of the stairs. Someone humming downstairs brought Samantha to a halt. Looking back at the room she had escaped from, she could've screamed with aggravation for not closing the door behind her. The hummer began to climb the creaky stairs.

Surprise—right now she did have the element of surprise working for her. Not daring to move in case the noise gave her away, Samantha waited. As the footsteps made their way slowly up the stairs, the stairs creaked with each step, her heart hammered louder and louder, and her breath came out in jagged spurts.

When whoever it was had almost reached the second floor, Samantha ran full tilt around the banister and launched herself off the top of the stairs, taking the camera guy with her. Hot coffee flew out of his cup and landed on Samantha's head as she drove the knife into his stomach. Their screams echoed off the empty walls. They flew backwards, never touching the stairs underneath them.

Samantha's eyes were level with the other guys, and she could see the shock and pain all rolled together.

When they hit the bottom of the stairs, they landed with a thud that sent Samantha scooting farther up onto the guy. She jerked her knife free and stood up, shaking the coffee out of her hair. The coffee felt like liquid fire as it dripped down into her eyes. Stumbling forward, her fingers fumbled with the locks on the door before she tore it open and stepped out into the freezing ice-cold wind that didn't bother her at all. She started running away from Pelo and his friend, heedless of where she might be running to.

Chapter Twenty

Running mad. This was New Orleans—bloody and dark and cold. It could be something or someone else's fault, but logically she held New Orleans accountable because every time she turned around in this town, she was running through the streets, waving a weapon like some mad person, who just escaped the nut house.

Skidding to a stop, Samantha shoved her knife into her boot and pulled her pants leg down. As soon as she got a chance, she was getting a second knife. The dim background light from a hat store did little to light up the dark street. Even the streetlights refused to cast enough light for anyone to feel comfortable about their safety. Most of the buildings in the area looked to be apartments with the exception of the hat store and the laundromat across the street. Her breathing leveled out as the fear and panic began to subside. The constant thud of her boots hitting the concrete sounded magnified on the desolate street.

Sky rises loomed ahead like a beacon in the darkness. At one of these damn hospitals in this city, she would find Jack, and that is exactly what she planned to do. Her mind skipped to Sam, but it was too painful. Maybe he was alive, and maybe he wasn't. That was about the best conclusion she had been able to come up with all week. One thing was for sure—Kevin was still alive, and he was going to stay that way.

What were the signs of hypothermia? Was it when the skin turned red or numbness of limbs? Holding her fingers up under a street lamp, she laughed out loud. Did blood count as redness? Probably not the type of redness she should be looking for. Stuffing her hands into her pants pockets, she trudged on until she reached a busy intersection.

The feel of the cash in her pocket gave her strength, and she raised her left hand to hail a cab. If she kept her right hand hidden, she might not look like the deranged lunatic she felt like. Maybe the cab driver would think she needed medical attention.

The first cab flew by her, causing Samantha to check her suit. For all she had been through, it wasn't covered with blood. Waving more wildly, the next cab pulled over and Samantha jumped in. "Nearest hospital please. Would you happen to know if it's the hospital near the Garden District?"

"Yeah, St. Vincent's. Right next to the Garden District. That's the one you want, huh?"

"That's the one." Sitting back in the cab, she closed her eyes and took a deep breath. She couldn't think about being tired. No, if this was going to work at all, she had a lot to do in a short amount of time. If she closed her eyes for just one minute....

"Hey, lady, you want a hospital or a motel room?"

Samantha sat up and handed two bills to the cab driver as the car stopped. Once she stepped out of the car, the cold wind helped to snap her out of the drowsiness left over from the drug. Forcing herself to enter the emergency room, the bright lights beat down on her, giving her a jarring headache. The nurse looked up at her, and Samantha nodded, striding by as if she had done this a hundred times before.

Her back bristled as she waited for someone to try to stop her, but the only sound she heard came from the click of her heels on the linoleum floor. Looming in front of her sat two elevators. She punched the up button before she realized it was her bloody right hand. Tucking it back in her pocket, she quickly checked to make sure no one had noticed. Nobody appeared in either hall, and, thankfully, the elevator door slid open.

Breathe and concentrate—the never-ending internal chant. The elevator chugged its way from the basement to the third floor. The only floor she knew for sure Jack wasn't on was the maternity ward. Why hadn't she asked the nurse downstairs? But of course, she didn't want to attract attention.

The elevator doors opened on the third floor, and a small family looked up and then away when they realized she had no news. Samantha glanced at the swinging double doors to her left and marched through them. A large circular unmanned desk made Samantha so happy she almost peed.

Fumbling through different stacks of papers on the desk, she gave up trying to find a chart or list of names. As she circled around the desk, her head twisted from side to side, but still no one walked around the corner. The computer glowed, and Samantha clicked on patients. A screen with a list of questions popped up. Name being the first question on the page. It hit her like a punch to the gut, causing a cold trickle of sweat to make its way down her back. She didn't know Jack's last name. He had mentioned it once when they were in Mexico. Samantha's mind flashed to the elegant hotel in Juarez when they had checked in, pretending to be boyfriend and girlfriend, but no last name popped into her head. She could tell you exactly what shade of brown his eyes were or how he threw a punch or even how many seconds between each of his snores, but his last name wouldn't come to her mind.

Typing in his first name, she entered yesterday's date and tried to console herself that she even knew that. Bingo, there were three Jacks admitted yesterday, but the name Brenner caught her attention. Clicking on his name, she found he was on the 5th floor. She zipped the mouse to the x at the top of the page, making sure she didn't leave a trail behind her, and scurried out from behind the circular desk.

The sound of soft rubber heels floated in the otherwise silent corridor. Samantha kept a steady pace, walking as fast as she could without drawing any attention to herself. Letting the doors swing shut, she ducked around the corner and punched the button for the elevator. The family hadn't moved since she last saw them. The mother continued to look through a magazine and the two daughters seemed intent on their handheld games or phones. The father stared at the ceiling, never bothering to turn his attention her way. The elevator dinged and Samantha slid in, sighing with relief as she pressed the button for the 5th floor.

Her foot tapped impatiently for the elevator to ramble up. The smell of antiseptic combined with the feeling of being stuck inside a metal box caused her chest to tighten. At least, the crappy lethargic feeling no longer impeded her every thought and movement. A flash of pain on the right side of her chest forced Samantha to take a deep breath in an attempt to control the panic. Rolling her eyes in agitation at herself, she made a quick promise to break down after she saved Jack and Kevin.

The elevator doors slid open, and she scanned the white walls for signs. Her eyes caught the piercing gaze of a male nurse, who sat behind the desk. "I'm sorry, but visiting hours are over. You're going to have to come back tomorrow."

She smiled, keeping her hands in her pockets as she stepped out of the elevator. "I know it's late, but I flew in from California. My brother, Jack Brenner, was in a car wreck today and this was the fastest I could get here. I did hear, however, that he made it through surgery. I was hoping to just have a quick peek before I try to get a hotel nearby." Stopping a foot away from the desk, she willed herself to keep her breathing steady. She was close to Jack; she could save him.

The nurse looked up at her with kind blue eyes, and Samantha felt her skin crawl. What if she had blood in her hair or on her face? She hadn't even stopped in a bath-room to check. Refusing to give into the impulse to shuffle her feet, she smiled and waited, hoping beyond hope that she could get a little luck.

"Five minutes. Do you know what room he's in?"

"518."

He nodded. "Straight down the hall. I just checked on him. He's heavily sedated, so don't try to wake him."

The ticking of the large clock accompanied by an occasional whir of a machine kept the corridor from a stifling silence. The hair on the back of her neck stood straight up, making her whole scalp burn. The nurse had recently checked on him, so maybe Samantha was overreacting. The hallway offered nothing but white walls and half-open doors. Of course, inside the rooms, the lights were out—so only about twenty rooms for a killer to hide in.

Samantha straightened her back and stopped in front of room 518. She took a deep breath and stepped inside. The only light came from the machines along the wall by Jack's bed. Her eyes adjusted to the darkness as she slowly moved closer, carefully placing her hand on his forehead.

He lay there without moving except for his rhythmic breathing. Bandages covered his neck and his hair stuck straight up as usual. The moonlight from the window made her believe that he didn't look too bad—with the lights off, anyway.

A single click brought her world to a complete halt. She turned, knowing exactly what she would find. He didn't have black spiky hair or a vulture's smile, but her nightmare stood inside the door with his gun pointed directly at her. She wished her killer would talk for hours, but she knew instinctually this guy would never say a word. The sound of a gun being fired with a silencer is like a whisper of deadly power. One minute a heart is beating, and the next minute it's not. Her killer hit the floor before he could ever fire a shot.

Samantha stared at the body on the floor and then at the man in the door. His blonde bangs hung to one side, and he wore a grin she remembered from a million childhood memories. Sam slipped his gun inside his jacket as he moved into the dark room out of the hall.

Chapter Twenty-One

For a moment, she stood perfectly still, gripping the bed railing for support. She felt lightheaded and dizzy as if she didn't trust the moment to be real.

"You going to stand there and cry, or are we getting out of here?"

"I'm not crying," Samantha said, brushing her shaking hand across one cheek and then the other. "I can't believe you're alive." She stepped over the feet of the dead gunman with rubbery legs and put her arms around Sam, hugging him hard enough to make sure he really existed. It felt good to hold on to him, so he couldn't disappear. The smell of soap and cigarettes reassured her that not everything in life was bad.

Sam gave her a bear hug, lifting her slightly off the floor. "We have to get out of here." He began pulling her by the hand towards the door of the hospital room, but Samantha drew back.

"Not without Jack," she hissed. In the dark room with only the hall light to illuminate him, Samantha could still see the whites of Sam's eyes when he rolled them back into his head.

He took a deep breath as if he might explode and strode over to where Jack lay sleeping. He unplugged the heart beat monitor and then pulled it off of Jack's finger. Removing the tape on Jack's arm caused him to jerk in his sleep a little, but he never bothered to wake up.

Samantha stood by the foot of the bed. Her mouth felt dry and her stomach did a quick flip as Sam removed the needle from the I.V. out of Jack's arm. Snapping his fingers to catch her attention, he motioned towards the door with his thumb.

Samantha grabbed onto the foot of the bed, and together they started angling the bed towards the door. Her mind froze. The realization that the body on the floor needed to be pushed aside hit her full force. Steeling herself against any qualms, she carefully stepped around the blood and picked up the guy's arms. Not daring to look at his mangled face, she managed to drag him out of the way.

Slowly, they pushed the bed around the body and out into the hall. Samantha tried to turn the bed to go back the way she had come, but Sam shook his head. He jutted his chin out for her to go in the opposite direction.

As the wheels made a slight squeaking sound in the deserted hall, Samantha kept waiting for someone to come storming down the corridor. They reached the service elevator, and with a shaking finger, she pushed the down button. Her heart pounded in her ears as she realized Jack's phone was probably back in the hospital room. She swung her head around, checking out the empty hall before she darted off, running on her tiptoes.

"No," she heard her brother whisper, but she didn't dare slow down. One, two, three, four, five, six doorways until she slid into the dark room. Nothing had moved (especially not the guy on the floor). Dragging her eyes away from the pool of blood, she darted to the closet and felt her panic decrease a notch when she wrapped her fingers around a plastic bag. Checking for the phone before running off again, she put her hand inside the bag and fished around for it. At the bottom of the bag underneath the shoes, holster and clothes, she wrapped her fingers around the only link she had to Kevin.

Footsteps in the hallway caused her to freeze. With quiet, quick movements, she sneaked behind the door. Of course, someone would come in any minute and find the dead guy on the floor, but instead of stopping, the soft pattering of rubber-soled shoes on the linoleum floor continued down the hall.

Samantha crept out from behind the door. The shrill ring of the phone made her almost drop the bag on the floor. She held her breath and rummaged in the bag. It didn't matter; she had to get out of here. Striding out of the room and down the hall, she cringed inwardly when a nurse stuck her head out of one of the rooms.

The nurse blinked a couple of times, before pushing up the spectacles carelessly situated at the end of her nose. "What are you doing here?"

Samantha smiled her best smile while the phone let out one last wail destroying every bit of sanity she had left.

"Is that a patient's bag?" The nurse's eyes narrowed, her mouth puckered and her ponytail bounced accusingly as she stepped out of the room, positioning herself as if to block Samantha's path.

"Yes it is." Samantha skirted around the nurse and continued to briskly walk towards the elevator. "My brother checked out but left his bag here. I can't stay because he has to have his insurance card to get his prescriptions."

"Young lady, you get back here this instant, or I'm calling security," the nurse's voice shook with anger.

Focusing on the closed doors of the elevator in front of her, Samantha's mind raced with what to do next. Sam and Jack must have taken the elevator down; maybe she should take the stairs. She turned to the left, breaking for the stairs as the doors of the elevator opened. Jack lay sleeping in his bed, and Sam glowered, waiting for her. Blowing out a breath, she jumped into the elevator.

Sam scowled at her and punched the button for the first floor.

"I'm calling security. You won't get out of this hospital without proper ID for that bag." The nurse's threat floated into the elevator before the doors could close.

"No possible way you could've not gone back for the bag?"

Samantha shrugged her shoulders. "I needed it. I have to save Kevin."

"Kevin is a patsy. No one can save him."

Samantha's face turned red. She could feel the anger rise up and start throbbing behind her temple. "You just don't like anyone I date."

The elevator stopped and the doors opened long enough for Samantha and Sam to come face to face with two security guards.

Sam pulled his gun out and pointed it at the guards while he pushed the button on the elevator, shutting the doors. "It's not that I don't like...." Sam took a deep breath and then laughed. "You're right. I don't like anyone you date, especially not a snitch."

The doors opened again onto the second floor. This time they both shoved on the bed, trying to get it out of the elevator. Sam waved his hand for Samantha to turn and go down the hall. She squeezed out and yanked on the bed, but the wheels refused to cooperate.

"Pick it up. Let's go."

"Why do I have to pick it up? He's heavy."

"You're the one who wanted to bring him along."

Samantha grabbed a hold of the bed and tried to lift. It barely budged, but when she put it down, the small movement caused the wheel to release.

They rolled down the hall as quickly as possible. The first door they came to Sam opened it, and they rushed inside. Quietly closing the door behind them, Samantha let out a sigh of relief, which died in her throat when someone in the room clicked on a light. Sam and Samantha stood petrified, staring at the pregnant woman who threw her covers off and attempted to roll out of the bed.

"Why are you barging in my room in the middle of the night?" The lady managed to swing her feet off the bed and onto floor.

"We have a bit of an emergency is all," Samantha stuttered, trying to stall for time. She glanced in Sam's direction, giving him the fix this now look. Even with his blonde hair covering one side of his face, his blue eyes sparkled with merriment. Adrenaline junkie—how could he think this was amusing?

The woman reached for her buzzer beside the bed.

"Don't call a nurse," Sam's voice carried a calm authority. "It's a police matter. This man is in a lot of danger, and we need to hide him for a few minutes.

Officers are making the rounds right now. We'll be able to move him shortly."

The woman's hand hovered over the button as she struggled to decide if they were legitimate. "Where's your badges?"

Samantha snorted. "We've been undercover for weeks. A lucky break sent us here minutes before his identity leaked. Can I fix your pillows for you or get you a glass of water?" Her attention wandered to the small leafy branch hanging above the woman's bed with miniature flip-flops hanging from it. Someone must have thought a little decoration would go a long way.

The woman shook her head. "I can't drink anything right now because the medicine will make me sick. They give me ice to suck on, but it's all right. This is my fourth." She patted her belly, which stuck out like a basketball. "At least, I get some rest before going home and dealing with the other three."

Nervously, Samantha reached up to pull her fingers through her hair, instantly dropping her hand. "I'm sorry to bother you, but I really have to use the bathroom." Without waiting for an answer from either of them, Samantha darted around Sam and closed the bathroom door. Crap, that could've been bad. She leaned against the door, willing herself not to shake. A quick look in the mirror relieved some of her tension. How she had managed to escape and not be covered in blood baffled her. If that lady had seen any of the blood on Samantha's hand, they would've been done for. She scrubbed her hands with soap, ignored the blood on the sleeve of her jacket and refused to put soap on her wrists. Then she scrubbed the soap and the sink to keep from leaving a bloody mess. A glass sat on the counter, and Samantha filled it, quickly guzzling the water. Her mind reeled so fast that she didn't know if any of this was a side effect of being drugged or a reaction to the pressure. The fact that she had to pee ranked high on the insanity list, but she didn't have a choice.

Returning to the room, Samantha glanced from the woman in the bed to Sam. He kept a straight face, but Samantha knew he teetered on the verge of skipping out. "Is there another way out of this place besides the elevators?"

The woman nodded. "Right next to my room, there's vending machines and a door that leads to a smoking patio. It's ..."

Before she could finish, Samantha cracked the door, peeking into the hall. With no sign of the security guards, she opened the door, and they hurried out of the room, whipping the bed into the vending area.

Breaking for the door, Samantha's heart pounded as she reached for the handle, hoping it wasn't locked. The door opened and the cool night air blew around her. Sam shoved the bed, practically knocking her out of the way. Sure enough a flight of stairs led down into a garden area. "What now?" Samantha squeaked, feeling her resolve to get Jack out of here leaking away.

"I'll get him. You get the bed."

"What?"

"Help me lift him! Do it right now, or I'm leaving."

Samantha grabbed one of Jack's arms, heaving him into a sitting position as Sam pulled his legs to the end of bed. With a whole lot of grunting, they hoisted Jack onto Sam's back. Sam took a couple of staggering steps forward and started down the stairs with Jack's feet dragging on the steps.

Samantha watched, holding her breath as the two of them wobbled from side to side. Each second increased their chances of getting caught. Did the guards pass by them while they hid in the lady's room? Finally, Sam and Jack reached the bottom of the stairs and got out of her path. She grabbed the bed, lining it up with the stairs.

Backing down the stairs, the idea that this appeared to be the most haphazard stunt yet didn't stop her from pulling the bed down the first step. For a second, she rocked on her heels, not knowing if she could hold the weight or if she'd end up flattened like a pancake under the bed. Five steps down she started to sweat. As her foot stepped down for the sixth step, the stupid plastic bag slipped off the bed. Samantha lunged to catch it, but the weight of the bed pushed her over. The bed bounced from step to step as Samantha watched in horror the chaotic descent. Jerking the bag up off the step, she raced down after the clanking, metal, soon to be heap. The bed reached the bottom and shot forward into the bushes lining the fence. Samantha spun around to find Jack sitting in a wheelchair with Sam holding his head up to keep it from falling to one side.

"You mean I didn't have to carry this bed down?"

"I'm not sure carry would be the correct term, but …"

The wail of a siren sliced through the argument. Samantha locked eyes with Sam. They both started running for the only exit they could see. Sam pushed Jack so fast Samantha cringed, hoping he didn't fly out of the wheelchair. The sliding glass door opened, and the three of them rushed into a brightly lit corridor. Slowing their pace, they walked as briskly as possible.

A male nurse at the emergency room desk immediately picked up a phone as soon as he saw them approach. Samantha could hear him mumble something about a man and a woman pushing a wheelchair towards the south emergency room exit. Doors to the outside opened, and at long last, they escaped out of the hospital.

"You take over. I'm going to get the car and pick you up. Keep heading towards the parking garage." Sam pointed straight ahead, and Samantha nodded as she started pushing the wheelchair. More sirens screamed into the night. The sound made the hair on the back of her neck stand up. Headlights flashed over her, and Samantha froze, not knowing whether to run, or not. The car pulled into the emergency lane, and the driver jumped out, running to assist the passenger out of the car. She closed her eyes so very thankful, but the moment shattered when someone in front of her yelled, "Stop right there."

They stood in the shadows of the building, not quite concealed by the overhead floodlight shining bright enough that Samantha knew they were security guards. Another car's headlights glared in her face, but this time the car slammed on its brakes, drawing up beside her. She yanked the backseat door open and turned to figure out what to do with Jack.

"Get in," Sam growled.

Before she could scoot to the far side of the car, Sam had pushed Jack in on top of her, folded his legs up to fit inside the car and slammed the door. Without slowing down, he jumped into the driver's seat and floored the car. They sped out of the parking lot, taking the first light on a yellow as they zipped to the left. Lights blurred as Sam immediately took a back street, throwing Samantha into the side of the door. For the first time since they had abducted Jack, Samantha took a hard look at Jack's face and then his neck. From the dim light of the passing street lamps, the bandage appeared white. At least, blood hadn't seeped through; maybe escaping with him was the right thing to do. Sam's driving sucked at the best of times. She closed her eyes when they took another turn too fast, but the sound of sirens began to grow distant.

After about ten nauseating turns, the car slowed down and then came to a stop. Samantha opened her eyes as a large warehouse door rolled up. The car lights flashed on stacks of large boxes as Sam drove in, shut off the lights and killed the engine. The warehouse door shuttered closed, cutting them off from the outside world.

Chapter Twenty-Two

Sam's lighter flickered in the blackness as he lit his cigarette and inhaled. Samantha sat perfectly motionless in the backseat with Jack's head in her lap. Placing her shaky hand on his forehead, she noticed Jack's breathing kept a steady rhythm. He felt a little clammy but not too hot or sweaty, considering the horrible escape from the hospital.

"So you're alive." Samantha finally broke the silence as she tried to piece together the last crazy hour of her life.

Sam chuckled. "Yeah, barely, and if you weren't such a stubborn pain in the ass, my plan would've worked beautifully."

"Oh, I am dying to hear this."

Sam took a drag of his cigarette and blew it out. "Well, I guess the short version is we embezzled money from José Guerrero, and I told Ani to kill me off and blame me for the embezzlement."

Samantha sat in stunned silence for a minute. "I don't get it. Why did you want to be killed off?"

"Simple really, I wanted a fake identity, so I could split. I didn't want to worry about people tracking me down. For the first time, I got cash and freedom. I wanted you to stay in the dark about most of it, so you could be convincing to the cops." Sam's voice took on a condescending tone, "You were supposed to stay with Lisa for a couple of weeks until things cooled off, and then the three of us were going to take off together."

"So you used me and it backfired."

"That's a bit of an understatement. You went completely AWOL."

"I watched my brother get blown to pieces, and I tried to escape without ending up dead."

"Escape.... What kind of escape places you right in the middle of a war?"

The car felt too small and too tight. He had no business making judgments. It was his stupid plan that put her in this mess in the first place. No, the crappy reality was she put herself here. Opening the car door, she carefully laid Jack's head on the back of the seat, before getting out of the car. The place smelled like stale dust. The thin jacket didn't keep the cold from seeping in. Samantha wrapped her arms around herself as she leaned against the car.

Sam turned on the headlights and got out, kicking a plastic container out of his way. It bounced a couple of times on the cement, before coming to a stop. He wrapped his arm around her shoulder and pulled her close to him. "I get it. It's been hard, but it's over. We have the money. Let's bail."

She stared at him, trying to grasp onto the implications of his words. This fake persona she had assumed over the last two weeks could be left behind. Turn back into Karen Cane and forget everything. Relief mixed with disbelief like oil and water. She couldn't abandon Jack, and she wouldn't abandon Kevin. But ...

The large door started rolling up. Samantha caught Sam's stony expression.

"Hide," he whispered, shoving her away from the car.

Panic raced through her as she darted around boxes, looking for a spot big enough to conceal her. Crouching behind a crate, she waited as a vehicle rolled into the warehouse.

"Hey, park over there," Sam shouted at the driver.

The engine shut off, and several doors slammed shut. Large overhead lights flickered on, and Becki's shrill voice filled the warehouse, "What the hell are you doing here?"

Samantha closed her eyes, silently cursing. If she had a gun, she would start shooting right now. How could this even be happening to her?

"I'm trying to clean up your sloppy mess. That guy you sent to the hospital botched up in a bad way. Jack killed him and would've got away if I hadn't been there to stop him."

Becki's head swung from Sam to the car. "Is he still alive?"

"Barely, I dropped in here to get a shovel. Hey, Steve, get me a shovel from over there. So how did you get lucky enough to nail Jack this morning, anyway?"

"I got a call from Sandra out at Cassie's place. She said Jack and Samantha had spent the night out there. Before ten this morning, they were parked outside my house in one of Cassie's cars no less."

While Becki talked, Sam motioned with his hand for Samantha to stay put. Her heart sunk, knowing Sam planned on leaving with Jack. As long as Becki didn't figure out Sam and Samantha were brother and sister, his story sounded convincing. The cramping started in her toes before Sam had even backed out of the warehouse. The aching spread up into her legs as the big door thumped back down. How long would she have to stay here in this dust factory?

Becki retrieved Samantha's shopping bag out of the SUV. She walked it over to an old couch and dropped it on floor. "Steve, you stay here. If Kevin shows up, shoot him. Max, take me home."

Seconds dragged on forever. Samantha put one hand behind her to help ease herself to the floor. Please get out of here she chanted. She was so close to her phone that the beating of her heart drummed in her head. Sweat ran down

239

the side of her face despite how cold she felt. As long as she didn't tremble—another minute and Becki would be gone. A single sneeze threatened to escape. It tickled the inside of her nose and throat. Quickly, Samantha brought her hand up to prevent herself from sneezing, but her fingers were now covered in dust. The sneeze echoed in the large warehouse.

"Search the place. It came from over there," Becki screeched. Her arms waved wildly in the air as if to make everyone around her speed up.

Samantha jerked her pants leg up and pulled her knife out. Some huge guy barreled over the crate and landed directly on top of her. The knife caught him in the stomach, but his weight pinned her to the ground, knocking the breath out of her. He rolled off of Samantha moaning and clutching his stomach as Steve drew his gun and pointed it at her.

Becki stood beside Steve grinning. "You keep trying, but the reality is you're not meant to live through the night. Max, get some rope."

"Drop the knife, or I shoot you in the knee for fun."

Steve resembled a scarecrow with his bushy blonde hair and thin frame. His eyes narrowed on Samantha, and she let the knife clatter to the concrete beside her.

Max came back with a really long piece of rope, knelt down beside her and seized her wrist. He glanced at her already bloody wrist, slid the rope around it and pulled so tight Samantha knew for sure she would lose her circulation. He snatched up her other hand and looped the rope around it. The sensation of the rope dragging across her already burned wrists made her turn her eyes water as she gritted her teeth.

"Now, now, don't worry. We'll put you out of your misery soon. Get her in the back of the SUV. I'm ready to go."

Max yanked on the rope, and Samantha scrambled to get up. He didn't slow down as he marched towards the big black vehicle, opened the back and nodded with his head. "Get in."

Clambering in, thoughts kept running through her head of how she could escape. Unfortunately, most of them involved men in big red capes. Maybe her brother would follow the SUV. Not likely. He'd come back here, expecting to find her hiding. Slumping down inside the cargo space of the SUV she kept her eye on Max in case he let go of the rope for half-a-second, but, of course, no such luck.

"Hurry up, Steve. I don't want to stand here, holding the rope all night."

Steve shouldered the guy with the stab wound over to the truck, helping him climb into the backseat. He darted around the SUV and jumped into the back next to the wounded guy. As soon as Max handed over the rope, Steve began to jerk on it. "We'll have some fun, won't we?" He leaned over the back of the seat, showing off a grin Samantha knew should be in a horror flick.

Becki finally cut off her phone conversation and climbed into the front passenger seat. "Drop Clyde off at a gas station. Tell them someone robbed you. If you utter anything different, Clyde, they'll never find your bones. What did you do with Pelo, Samantha? I can't get a hold of him."

"Last time I saw him he was still alive. If someone killed him since because they mistook him for road kill, it's not my fault."

"Everything is your fault. Now shut up before I have Steve put some sense into that little head of yours."

Samantha sat in the back, pondering if things really were her fault. Where did she go wrong? Did it start when Ani supposedly killed Sam? Was it the moment she grabbed the gun in self-defense? Or maybe it was when she ran to Eddie for help. He ended up getting killed because she wasn't able to protect him. If it all came down to a single event, could it go as far back as the time in grade school when the teacher caught Sam stealing twenty bucks, and she had covered for him. All of that didn't matter. The feel of the cold, bloody, sticky, wet shirt pressed against her skin made her want to claw it off.

The SUV stopped at a red light. Samantha poked her head up to see if there were any other cars. A cop car sat right behind them at the light. With a shaky finger, she wrote help on the back window; then she started pounding on the window and yelling as loud as she could. The backhand came fast and hard. Steve hit her square in the side of the head. She landed on the floor, listening to the ringing in her ear and the muffled voice coming from Steve's mouth.

"Keep it up, girly. I'm just getting started with you," Steve said as he jerked viciously on the rope.

Samantha tried not to whimper, but the rope bit into her wrists unmercifully. The SUV turned into a parking lot. Steve climbed over Clyde, opened the door for him and pushed him out. The rope remained firm in Steve's hand the entire time, forcing Samantha to scoot from one side of the SUV to the other. They sped out of the lot, making enough turns to cause Samantha to slide all the way down onto the floor to avoid getting tossed around. Checking under the seat and along the floor for anything that might work as a weapon, she found a gum wrapper and a used up sucker stick. Hey, maybe she could poke someone's eye out. She tried gnawing on the rope with her teeth, but Steve caught her and jerked her arms high enough to lift her shoulders and back completely off the floor; then he dropped her with a thud.

Every minute felt like an eternity as Samantha lay on the floor, wondering if she had half a chance in hell of getting out of this mess. Sam probably knew Becki had abducted her by now, but what good would it do her if he couldn't find her?

The SUV came to a sudden stop. One of the front doors opened, and Samantha heard someone climbing out of the truck.

"Get rid of her, and go back to the warehouse. I don't want to miss Kevin because we can't handle his newest toy. If I had more time, Samantha, I'd let Kevin find you like he did Evie ... oh well."

The door slammed, and the SUV took off. At least now, the odds were two to one. It sounded good but didn't feel any better as she bounced around on the floor. This time they got on the freeway. The lack of streetlights and the fact that they didn't have to come to any stops clued her in, but the knowledge only made it difficult to breathe. Everything had turned into a black pit of death. It didn't even matter that Steve would kill her. Death had already arrived. Fear, fear of everything: fear of lying on a dirty SUV floor, fear of a bloody shirt sticking to her skin, fear of a darkness sweeping ever closer.

"Looks like little queen Becki forgot her purse."

"I'm not going back. She can come and get it tomorrow. We have to take care of this little darlin' right now." Steve grinned as he gazed over the seat at Samantha.

Wanting to become invisible, Samantha scooted deeper into the shadows behind the seat. Something about Steve made her almost miss Pelo (hairy back included).

"We can drag this one, right?" Steve whined as he finally turned his head back to the front.

"Man, you don't give up."

"Last time you said this time, and we got the rope."

The word drag made her think he wanted to throw her out of the truck. Now what kind of sick twisted moron would come up with that one?

The SUV left the freeway for a pitch-black, dirt road. With her fingers, she tried picking at the rope, anything to get away, but her hands had been tied so tightly, she only succeeded in creating more rope burns on her wrists.

"Come on, Max, you said that next time ..."

Max slammed on the brakes, threw his door open and marched around to the back. He lifted the hatch and reached in to grab Samantha's legs. She kicked him in the face as hard as possible. Steve started yanking on the rope, but Samantha kicked Max anywhere she could: the head, the gut. She barely missed his groin as he leaped to the side.

"If you want her out so bad, you do it," Max shouted. He stomped back to the driver's side, started the truck and hit the accelerator.

Steve leaned over the seat and began pushing Samantha out of the SUV. She bit his ear and wacked him with her bound hands. He screeched and punched her, but when he did, his efforts forced him to lean over the backseat.

Samantha groped inside his jacket and found exactly what she needed. Not having any space or any time, she quickly fired the gun at him. Steve crumpled instantly. Jerking the gun out from under him, Samantha heard another shot go off. This time a bullet streaked right past her head. She fired at Max, hitting him in the back of the skull.

Fate is twisted. Samantha never doubted her complete and utter inability to overcome her fate no matter how hard she tried. The SUV shot forward, knocking Samantha out of the back. In that moment as she fell backwards out of the truck, the clear insight of her being tied to Steve hit her full force. The two idiots were most likely dead, yet even from the grave, they held her with the unyielding grip of Death, himself. She watched the free fall to the ground, knowing she couldn't keep the inevitable from happening. Samantha fired the gun directly at the rope. She hit the ground. Everything went black.

Chapter Twenty-Three

A loud crashing sound rang in her ears as Samantha lay perfectly still. The pain pounded unrelenting in the back of her head. Forcing herself to open her eyes, she blinked, not quite sure of anything. Large trees reached with gnarled branches above her head to block as much of the sky as possible. Pushing herself up to a sitting position, nausea swept through her. Overcome with the urge to puke, she swung her hanging head to one side. Everything she had been holding in came out until nothing was left. The cold wind struck her hot and clammy skin, giving her the shakes.

Little by little her senses began to return. The smell of wet dirt penetrated her brain when she realized she sat in the middle of a muddy road. Twenty yards ahead the SUV leaned into a ditch with the driver's side of the vehicle crushed up against the bank.

Half-crawling, half-stooping, she staggered towards the truck. Inside some guy's head rested against the steering wheel. As she reached for the door handle, Samantha changed her mind and let her hand drop to her side. Even if the SUV still ran, she didn't have the strength to lever the guy out of the way. On teetering legs, Samantha began walking down the road in the direction of the highway. The only light came from the moon, breaking through the clustered tree branches above the road. The gun looked more like a large rock, but instinctually, she bent over to pick it up. Dizziness rushed through her, making her fall onto her knees as she grasped the weapon. With her hands still tied together, she stuffed the gun into her pants, rose slowly to her feet and meandered down the road.

The crunch of the gravel under her boots didn't drown out her whirling thoughts. Karen Cane.... Could she turn back into her? If Samantha Cross didn't exist, what would happen to Sam and Jack and Kevin? Walk away.... Walk away.... Something didn't add up. A spark flitted around the edges of a memory. Flashes of faces danced in her thoughts. Something to do with her brother and Becki made a buzzing noise in her head. Her boots grew heavier as she trudged down the muddy road. Along with the dizziness and pounding head, she had begun to notice an ache in her back as if her vertebras had been pulled apart and shoved back together.

Headlights flashed. Samantha wanted to hide behind the trees, but a vision of her laying frozen dead on the ground forced her to stay in the middle of the road. She needed help. What would they think with her hands tied together and a gun sticking out of her pants? Standing in the middle of the road, she began to lift and lower her arms in the hopes of flagging them down.

The car slowed and then stopped. The driver got out and ran to her. She blinked in disbelief as Kevin dragged her to him, holding her shaking body against him. Closing her eyes, she felt her legs give out underneath her as relief swept through her.

"Did you get shot or stabbed?" He steadied her and then took a step back, supporting her with his hands while he inspected her.

Samantha glanced down as if she didn't know either. The headlights from the car revealed an ugly red stain all over her pants, shirt and jacket along with blood splatters that covered the top half of her outfit. "No, but ..." She held up her hands.

"What happened to Becki?" he asked while he guided her to the car, opened the passenger door and helped her to get in. Bending down, he started untying the rope.

"Long gone," Samantha mumbled.

"I met up with Sam and Jack at the warehouse. They told me Becki had kidnapped you."

"Jack?" Samantha tried lifting her head. The words slipped from her thoughts, and she let her head roll to the side.

"Yeah, I convinced Sam to drive Jack out to Cassie's."

Samantha sat up suddenly rigid. "That's no good. It's no good, Kevin. Someone's a snitch. Someone snitches for Becki. You're a snitch," Samantha blurted as she stared into his dark blue eyes unable to control her words or thoughts. "I love you."

Kevin stopped removing the rope and cocked his head to look directly in Samantha's eyes. He reached up, gently running his fingers down her cheek. "I think you have a concussion. Will you marry me?"

Samantha smiled and leaned against the seat. Everything about him was so beautiful: the way he smelled like the ocean or a cool breeze, his dark eyelashes and curly brown hair. Of course, she would marry him in just one minute. Right after she rested her eyes. Against her will the lids of her eyes started closing. She needed to say yes, but maybe in a minute …

Carefully slipping off the last of the rope, he pulled her seatbelt over her, clicked it into place and closed the door. When he got in the car, he shook her. "You can't go to sleep on me."

She grinned and nodded. No, not sleep…. Here comes the bride, but a nauseous feeling came back when the car started forward. Samantha felt like she was suffocating. At the exact moment sleep drug her into unconsciousness, Kevin shook her. He kept shaking her, and she wanted to hit him. The damn car made her sick if only she could get out into the freezing night air. She rolled down her window, letting the cold air hit her in the face.

Finally, they stopped, and Samantha opened her eyes. Kevin helped her out of the car, keeping his hand wrapped around her waist as he supported her inside and up the stairs.

Samantha's mind registered tile stairs that went on forever in an unending circle, each step getting them no closer to the top. Stumbling down a short hall, Kevin led her into a bedroom, sat her in a chair and began to undress her. "Since you can't go to sleep, we better get you cleaned up."

Samantha tried to narrow her eyes at him, but the effort was lost on him.

He maneuvered her into the shower, which surprisingly made some of her senses comeback. The first thing she realized was that he still had his clothes on even though he was dripping wet from the shower.

"I feel better," she said as he dumped shampoo into her hair.

"You had me pretty scared on the ride over here." He rubbed the shampoo in, before tilting her head backwards into the water.

As he dried her off, she noticed the yellow fluffy towel didn't remind her of a hotel. "Where are we?"

"It's one of Carlos's houses."

She squinted, trying to process the confused thoughts spinning around and around in her head. "I thought you went to Mexico."

"I did for about five minutes, but I decided no one would look for me in New Orleans. Plus, by then, I knew you were here." He wrapped a white terry cloth robe around her, and led her into the bedroom. "Are you going to go to sleep on me?"

Samantha shook her head no, regretting the movement as pain exploded behind her eyes. "I don't feel as rough as I did."

"Keep talking. I'm going to change clothes."

Sitting on the bed, she didn't know where to begin. Faces floated in her head, each one drumming up a barrage of questions. "What's Lisa's real name?"

The silence from the other room spoke volumes.

Kevin came back in, wearing boxers. He took a chair across from her and sat down. His blue eyes bore into her. "Her real name is Lexi Hearn."

"So you didn't kill her?"

"It's hard to have killed someone that's still alive."

Samantha stared back at him. She didn't want the nauseous feeling to return, but she needed to know.

"They offered Lexi the witness protection program as long as I agreed to help them bring down José Guerrero."

Kevin went into the bathroom and came back with some antiseptic. "This will definitely sting."

"Ha, sting, funny. So the detective that's been following me around, how does he play into this? Ouch, crap, that hurts."

Kevin knelt on the carpet and blew on her wrist. "I'm his only witness in the case he's been building against José Guerrero. He can't afford to lose me."

"And he doesn't know where you're at?"

"Not right now. When everyone around me started dying off, I figured I needed to go into hiding."

Samantha shook her red, raw wrists. "Why didn't Sam come with you to get me? How did you find me?"

Kevin smiled and looked sad at the same time. "I followed the tracker in Becki's purse. I lied to Sam and Jack. Told them I would go to José's estate and try to find Becki." He paused watching Samantha thoughtfully. "Sam can't go there because José thinks he's dead."

"But why lie?" She knew Kevin expected her to get it on her own, but thinking took more effort than she felt like exerting. Yes, she knew…. As he started to speak, the cold dread crept through her like a wild fire of freezing ice.

"I'm pretty sure Sam, Lisa, Becki and Ani stole the twenty-two million from Sal and Brody. They wanted me to take the rap for it. I never told you this because it made me sick, but about three weeks ago, Ani came to me and insisted Sam had stolen close to a million from José. I was the one who ordered Ani to kill Sam. Only, they faked it to leave a trail straight to me." He stood up and stretched. "Are you hungry?"

Samantha didn't know. Food didn't seem to be high on the list right now. "Maybe not."

"Are you supposed to drink anything if you have a concussion?"

She shrugged her shoulders.

"Here take a couple of sips. Your eyes really do look a lot better."

Samantha sipped the water. Sleep, if only, she could sleep for a little while.

"Come on, let's get some rest. I think I'm supposed to wake you up every hour."

Samantha crawled in bed next to Kevin, not caring if she ever woke up. In her dreams everyone wore white dresses, but Kevin kept interrupting by shaking her and forcing her to answer one stupid question after another. What's your name? Who am I? What's your brother's name?

Chapter Twenty-Four

The room reminded her of a resort somewhere in the tropics with bright yellow walls and dark furniture. A fantasy of being on vacation with Kevin played out in her head before she gathered the nerve to sit up. Very slowly, she rose up, making an internal diagnosis. The dizziness had passed, leaving a painful soreness in her back and wrists. The pounding headache appeared to be par for the course. Gingerly touching the side of her face, she crossed her fingers that the swelling and bruising wouldn't be as bad as the last time she got knocked around. Sadly enough being shot at, hit and now kidnapped was starting to become commonplace.

On the dresser she found a fruit plate, a glass of orange juice and a note.

I guess these are your clothes. I like the wig. I'll be back shortly.

Love, Kevin

Love ... first he rescues her. Well kind of ... and now love. She rummaged through the bag and extracted the orange silk dress. Every vacation needed suitable attire. Sliding it over her head, she yelped when the long sleeves touched her wrists. Very carefully, she rolled the sleeves up a little, so they wouldn't touch the burned skin. The mirror reflected an almost fragile pale blonde, wearing an orange silk dress. Fragile didn't usually describe her. Out of curiosity, she picked up the wig and arranged it around her face, so the blonde hair didn't poke out. The bruises didn't look as severe as the ones from last time. Steve might have been a mean, crazy, wild-haired scarecrow, but he didn't leave bruises. Now Max on the other hand. The deep red marks on her wrists stood out in bold contrast to the soft white skin of her hands and arms.

The door opened, and Samantha turned expecting to find Kevin. Instead the detective that had followed her all over New Orleans yesterday stood in the doorway. "Oh, I must have the wrong room," he muttered as he closed the door.

Samantha's breath escaped her in a silent whoosh. If she reacted quickly enough, maybe she could escape. Sliding her feet into her boots, she jerked her new coat on and shoved her phone and money into the pockets. Barreling for the sliding glass doors, she tore it open, peeked over the balcony and gripped the railing with both hands. Karen Cane … Samantha Cross … it didn't matter, but she wasn't going to play snitch. Kicking her legs over the metal rail, she dropped straight down.

Go to Colleensugden.com for updates on Samantha Cross Novels, and don't forget to pick up a copy of 'Hatchet Man' to find out how Samantha Cross became a hitman.

Hatchet Man

Time waited for her. If he had a gun, he never bothered to pull it out. She could've done a number of things different, but pivotal moments are defined by determining direction or effect. Her bullets hit him again and again. Karen Cane died with her brother, but Samantha Cross lived.

Made in the USA
Charleston, SC
09 March 2011